She reluctantly

"I wouldn't have take~~n the job if I'd known you~~ were coming back." Even with Caleb's sobs in her ear, Jonah's low voice cut through her.

She winced. Well, that put her in her place. It was her fault though. She'd done a good job of ensuring he'd felt that way before she'd left. *Leave them before they leave you.*

"I wouldn't have come back if I'd known you'd taken the job." Nausea threatened to spew out the moment the words left her mouth. But even if she could, she wouldn't take the words back. Better to keep him at arm's length. She'd come back to repair her reputation and relationships. Except this one. This one would best remain fractured.

A muscle flexed in his jaw. "Well, you can remedy that. Last time I heard, the bus goes both ways."

She widened her eyes to keep the burning at their backs at bay. She didn't intend to go back. But, with him in the house, could she now stay?

Publishers Weekly bestselling author **Jocelyn McClay** grew up on an Iowa farm, ultimately pursuing a degree in agriculture. She met her husband while weight lifting in a small town—he "spotted" her. After thirty years in business management, they moved to an acreage in southeastern Missouri to be closer to family when their oldest of three daughters made them grandparents. When not writing, she keeps busy grandparenting, hiking, biking, gardening, quilting, knitting and substitute teaching.

Books by Jocelyn McClay

Love Inspired

The Amish Bachelor's Choice
Amish Reckoning
Her Forbidden Amish Love
Their Surprise Amish Marriage
Their Unpredictable Path
Her Unlikely Amish Protector
The Amish Spinster's Dilemma
Her Scandalous Amish Secret

Visit the Author Profile page at LoveInspired.com.

Her Scandalous
Amish Secret

Jocelyn McClay

LOVE INSPIRED
INSPIRATIONAL ROMANCE

LOVE INSPIRED®
INSPIRATIONAL ROMANCE

ISBN-13: 978-1-335-59853-0

Her Scandalous Amish Secret

Recycling programs
for this product may
not exist in your area.

Love Inspired
22 Adelaide St. West, 41st Floor
Toronto, Ontario M5H 4E3, Canada
www.LoveInspired.com

Printed in U.S.A.

Trust in the Lord with all thine heart;
and lean not unto thine own understanding.
In all thy ways acknowledge him,
and he shall direct thy paths.
—*Proverbs* 3:5–6

Again and always, I thank God for this opportunity. I thank my husband, Kevin, for his patience, and Genna, for her encouragement while I was writing this story. This one is dedicated to fellow authors Karen and Shaen. Writing can be a solitary endeavor and it is such a joy to get together with you two.

Chapter One

Lydia Troyer straightened her shoulders as she felt the stares drilling through the pleats of her prayer *kapp*. She wasn't surprised. She deserved them. Still, it took considerable effort to swallow past the lump lodged in her throat, the one that'd been growing since last night when the bus had dropped her at the hamburger joint that served as the stop for Miller's Creek. Carefully lowering herself onto one of the hard backless benches that lined the central room of the house where this week's church was held, she took her seat amongst the other unmarried women of the community.

When her bottom lip threatened to quiver, she bit into it. The lump had been growing for far longer than just yesterday. Shame, homesickness, anguish and contrition had all contributed to it over the past year until it seemed almost as big as the Amish barns that dotted this part of the Wisconsin countryside.

But whereas those barns were usually white, her past was much darker. Lydia dropped her gaze as her throat bobbed again. And these people knew it. She pressed her hand against the nausea that flared in her stomach. Just, not all of it. Not the worst. Which was why she was back.

The shuffling of feet and creaking of wooden benches on the opposite side of the room announced the unmarried men had entered. *He* would be among them. Squeezing her eyes closed, Lydia drew in a ragged breath. She'd have to face him sometime. She just wasn't ready. *Will I ever be?* In such a small community it would be difficult to avoid him though. She'd see him on church Sundays, of course. But as long as she didn't socialize with the *youngies* and limited it otherwise in the district...

Ensuring her tension wasn't echoed in her hand, she gently stroked the back of the sleeping child cradled against her shoulder. Inhaling the sweet scent of clean baby, she rested her cheek on his downy head. Though her heart still raced, she slowed her breathing to match the slumbering cadence of his. He normally brought her tranquility. But today her mind was anything but peaceful.

His presence would raise questions she didn't have answers for. Quite a switch for someone with her reputation. A bead of sweat trickled down her back. *Please don't let folks discover the truth. At least not all of it.* Careful not to disturb the sleeping baby, she shakily exhaled. *I should be well acquainted with gossip, after the amount of it I've spewed. And now, I'm the topic. What goes around, comes around.* Lifting her gaze, she found several looks from the young women in the surrounding area pointed in her direction. None were openly hostile—at least not in church—and a few even looked sincere. All were curious.

"And who is this?"

Though Sarah Raber's whisper was accompanied with what appeared to be a sincere smile, Lydia flinched.

Licking dry lips, she considered the history she'd come home to address. Sarah had reason not to be friendly. Her family had been one of Lydia's previous targets. Lydia knew all the nearby young women had their ears tuned so sharply that they could probably hear a mouse squeak in the nearby barn. She forced a smile though her mouth felt stiff as concrete.

"His name is Caleb."

"Oh, that's right." Sarah's brow lowered in sympathy. "Your cousin's boy. I'd heard about her passing. How is her *mamm* doing?"

Lydia pressed what little fingernails she had into her palm to stifle the prickling that threatened behind her eyes. "She's a *wunderbar* woman." Lydia saw Sarah's gaze shift to the *boppeli* in her arms. "She was the one who suggested I come home with Caleb." That part was true at least.

"Well." Sarah gave her another smile as the *vorsinger* called out the page number of the first hymn. "I'm sure your family, and others in the community, are glad you're back."

Her smile wavering, Lydia nodded. Though she turned her attention to the *Ausbund* hymnal the girl held open between them, she ached to search the benches on the far side of the room for a certain dark-haired young man. There was one, at least, who she very much doubted was glad she'd returned.

She was back. Jonah Lapp's heart was pounding. His fingers clutched so tightly on his thighs, the weave of his pants' fabric was probably imprinted on their tips.

Of all the women in the district, of all those in the surrounding area, why was she the one to tempt him so? He knew better. Still, he couldn't pull his gaze away.

She looked different. As before, her red hair was sleeked back to disappear neatly into her *kapp*. But the Lydia who'd left last year, instead of lowering her gaze, would've been flirtatiously batting her dark blue eyes toward any man bold enough to meet them. Jonah scowled. She probably had this morning already; he just hadn't caught her. She'd done that before. Looked at him, and when she knew she had his attention, with a coy smile, flicked her gaze to another male nearby. A muscled twitched in his jaw at the memory.

He studied her with hooded eyes. Her face was thinner. Jonah lowered his brow. *She* was thinner. Was she ill? Frowning at the twist in his stomach at the possibility, he glanced down to jerk at a thread in the seam of his pants.

What was wrong with him? He had more sense than this. He should've forgotten her by now. She'd left. They'd said she wasn't coming back. That was the only reason that he'd… Resentment rippled through him. He *had* forgotten her.

But at his first glimpse today, his heart had

surged, his breath had caught and all his irrational longings had returned. She was more beautiful than before. Another thing to resent her for, something else to pick at his brain. And he didn't need another thing to worry about. He'd enough as it was with determining whether to go out on his own or stay at the farm when his *daed* refused to consider any improvements to the business.

Jonah glanced down the bench where he sat with the other unmarried men of their district. His nostrils flared when he saw his wasn't the only attention focused on Lydia. He snorted. And why would it be?

Although it'd felt like getting kicked in the belly by a shod horse, it hadn't surprised him to see her with a *boppeli*. His illogical turmoil had eased when he'd overheard—Jonah's ears reddened at his blatant eavesdropping—a conversation relating that it was a cousin's child. The girl who'd abruptly died in Pennsylvania, where Lydia had been staying for the past year.

He'd cocked an eyebrow at the news that Lydia had taken on the baby. She'd historically been more selfish than that. Having the little one would hamper her favorite pastime. Jonah's lips twisted. He knew her faults, knew her qualities, few though they be. And he'd loved her anyway.

More fool he.

"Lydia's back. You know what that means." The whisper behind him was followed by muffled snickers.

Clamping his arms across his chest, Jonah leaned forward to put distance between him and the sniggering *youngies*. Under the admonishing glare the commotion had engendered from the *vorsinger*, Jonah mouthed the words of the slow hymn, but his mind was far from the song that'd been sung second in Amish church services for centuries.

Though it hurt, he wouldn't have been shocked to discover the *boppeli* was hers. Lydia had given herself often and easily here in Wisconsin. Why should that have changed when she went to Pennsylvania? He just wished she hadn't given herself to him. And that he hadn't made the mistake of thinking it'd meant something. Hunching his shoulders against the heat that rose up the back of his neck, Jonah dropped his gaze. Uncrossing his arms, he concentrated on flexing fingers from his clenched fists one by one.

Ach, she'd made sure he hadn't lingered long under that misconception.

Blowing out a slow breath, he lifted his eyes

and scanned the row of unmarried women, this time bypassing Lydia to settle on a brunette who met his gaze with a raised eyebrow and smile. His shoulders relaxing fractionally, Jonah lifted his lips in an answering one. This was where his future should lie. He'd made mistakes in his past. He wasn't one to repeat them.

With gritted teeth, he battled the desire that threatened to pull his attention, like a magnet to steel, back up the row of young women, back to the redhead with the *boppeli*.

Lydia could tell from the way the minister's voice strengthened and sped up that he was wrapping up the sermon. Her *daed* had gotten better at them in the year she'd been gone. Henry Troyer had been as surprised as anyone when he'd been selected as a church leader. Not that he wasn't a *gut* man, he was. It was too bad she wasn't more like him than her mother. Lydia ducked her head. His improvement in preaching was probably because it was easier to face a congregation as a minister without her around. At least her *daed* wasn't the deacon, who assisted the bishop in disciplinary tasks. Wouldn't that have put him in a difficult position.

Under lowered lashes, she glanced beyond

the married men on the opposing benches to the younger ones seated farther back. Her gaze touched on the faces as she went down the row. She'd kissed him. And him. And done much more than that with him. Her mouth tightened as heat rose up her cheeks. And him. And with him…she inhaled sharply as she locked eyes with Jonah. Stiffening, she dropped her gaze. When Caleb stirred against her shoulder, she lightly patted his bottom, comforting them both.

With Jonah, she'd given everything. And for just a moment, had hoped everything. She'd forgotten her conviction. *Always leave them before they leave you. That way, it doesn't hurt as much.* Lydia carefully swallowed as Caleb, settling in again, nuzzled against her neck. At least, that was the philosophy. Obviously not an accurate one. Because it'd hurt anyway.

"I'm surprised to see you working in here instead of attending to some task where you'd be out there." Ruth Schrock nodded her head toward the window over the sinks as she briskly rubbed a dish towel over a plate.

Lifting her gaze from the soapy water, Lydia glanced out the window to where the young men and a few young women were taking advantage of the early fall weather to gather outside in small groups following the Sunday meal. She set another plate in the drainer. "I asked to work in the kitchen."

Ruth's eyebrows rose until they almost reached the auburn hair that swept back under her *kapp*. Lydia wasn't surprised. The year-ago Lydia would've requested any task that had her mingling with the men. *If* she'd requested any tasks at all. Her fellow dishwasher eyed Lydia speculatively. Bracing herself, Lydia held her gaze. She blinked when Ruth gave a slight nod.

"How old is the little one? About eight months?"

Under the surface of the sudsy water, Lydia's hand tightened on the edge of a plate. "There about," she replied hoarsely. The woman must've caught one of her many looks toward the stairway, from where young voices floated down. After the service, Lydia had reluctantly relinquished Caleb to the young girls stationed in one of the upstairs bedrooms. When his tiny brows had furrowed over concerned green eyes at the exchange, Lydia, stifling a sniff, had almost changed her mind and snatched him back. Outside the room, she'd paused, waiting to hear his cry. When there'd been nothing more than the girls' cheerful voices and soft gibberish of little ones, she descended the stairs, crossing her arms to alleviate their emptiness.

"I'm sure he's fine. As middle children with several younger siblings, I know the girls are well familiar with little ones and will take *gut* care of them. If I didn't believe so, I wouldn't leave my *dochter* with them. Although," Ruth said with a grin, "they probably wouldn't thank me for it. Deborah seems to have reached the terrible part without reaching the two part. I don't know where she gets it. Must be from her father."

Lydia smiled faintly. As far as someone to work beside, she could've done a lot worse today than Ruth Schrock. Although blunt, the woman didn't seem judgmental. But Ruth, a few years older than her, had never been the subject of Lydia's gossip and might not've been aware that Lydia had chased after her husband, Malachi, before Ruth married him.

When she'd taken her place at the sink to wash the piles of resale-shop china as they were returned to the kitchen, many sideways glances had greeted her from the women manning the area. But Lydia kept her head down and her attention on the plates and silverware moving in and out of the soapy water and was soon ignored. It was a good place.

With her focus on the sink, she didn't have to face the young men congregating outside. Nor the young women weaving throughout the crowd who'd previously been particular targets of her venom.

Besides, listening to the babble as women bustled around her, Lydia discovered doing dishes was a good way to catch up on what was going on in the community. Who'd died, who'd had babies, who'd planted a lot of celery in their garden and the speculation of whether it was because the homeowner liked that much celery, or did they have a *dochter* who might be anticipating a wedding?

"Are you all right?"

Lydia jolted at Ruth's voice at her elbow. "*Ja.* I'm fine. I… It just slipped." Fishing in the water, she found the plate she'd dropped when Jonah's name was mentioned.

"Careful. It might have broken."

Brushing suds from the plate, Lydia examined it. "*Nee.* It looks *gut.*" Fortunately the china hadn't cracked. Not like hearts easily did.

She was down to the last few dishes when the sound of male laughter floated in through the open window. A ripple went up her spine at the sound. Lydia focused her attention on scrubbing the pan used for the ham served for sandwiches that day. *I'm not going to look. I'm not going to look.* But she did. To see Jonah with Rebecca Mast, standing together, their bodies tipped toward one another, their faces smiling. Sinking her teeth into her lower lip, Lydia returned her attention to the pan.

"I'm a believer that cleanliness is next to godliness, but there won't be anything left of that pan the way you're working away on it. You keep it up, we'll have to take it over to Thomas Reihl's blacksmith shop and have him add some metal back to it." With a hooked eyebrow, Ruth held out her hand for the container.

Jerking the pan from the dishwater with a splash, Lydia rinsed it. "I just...wanted to do a *gut* job."

"I'd say you did." Ruth leisurely dried the roasting pan as she eyed her. When Lydia didn't respond, she shrugged. "I'd also say, as I don't recognize the cry, that your little boy is a mite unhappy. Either that or my Deborah is terrorizing someone."

"Oh." Whirling from the sink, Lydia swiped her hands down her apron to dry them and hurried toward the wailing that echoed down the stairs. It was indeed Caleb, who gave a watery gulp of relief at the sight of her. She swept him into her arms, relishing the warm weight of him.

"He'd been fine. I think he just decided he was missing you," one of the young attendants assured her.

"I'd been missing him, so I guess we're even." As Caleb buried his damp face against her neck, she rubbed his back in slow circles. "I think he's telling me it's been a big few days for him." It had for her too. And not only because of the travel from Pennsylvania.

After a quick search failed to locate her *daed* in the house, she strode to the barn, hoping to find him there. So direct was her focus on her destination, she might as well have worn blinders like a horse. Even so, she could measure the district's interest in her return by the conversations that paused at her approach and started again in her wake. To her relief, she found her *daed* in the shade of the open barn, talking with a few other farmers regarding the fall's harvest.

Her shoulders relaxed imperceptibly when he greeted her with a smile.

"I need to go... I'd like to take him home." She dipped her chin toward Caleb, who was gazing at the barn's interior with wide eyes.

"*Ja.* I suppose so." Nodding to his associates, Henry exited the barn with Lydia following in his wake. As everyone called out farewells to the minister, it was a slow process. Although they spoke to her *daed*, their eyes were on her and Caleb. It seemed more like hours than minutes before her *daed* finally collected his horse and led him into the field lined with rows of black buggies.

Lydia's shoulders sagged in exhaustion as they reached their own. She'd made it. It was only one day, but still, better than she might've expected it to be. Although she wouldn't always, today she'd managed to avoid several of the folks she'd hurt, including the one she least wanted to face.

She froze when a man emerged from the buggy beside them with a blue-and-white volleyball in his hand.

"Jonah." Her *daed* clapped the young man's shoulder. "I haven't been able to get to the house the past few days before you left. I wanted to tell you that you're making *gut* progress." Henry turned from the rigid form beside him to Lydia. "Guess I haven't had a chance to mention it in the bustle since you've returned, though you might've noticed the change. I've decided to add on a *daadi haus* to our place and Jonah here has been doing a fine job on the carpentry work."

Chapter Two

Lydia was sure she was as white as the prayer *kapp* that rested on her head. At her tightened grip, Caleb pushed back from her shoulder to peer at her. When he looked from her set face to the man staring at her, his erupting wail splintered the tense silence.

Automatically, Lydia rubbed the boy's back to soothe him. Though still voicing his concern, Caleb's crying subsided at her touch. Her breath escaped with a shudder. Any reassurance for *her* was elusive. The one person she'd hoped to avoid upon her return would be working in her home.

Whirling to her father, she shifted Caleb to the shoulder away from the dark-haired man. Even now out of sight, his stiff, unsmiling presence loomed larger than the huge barn they'd recently left.

"A *daadi haus*?" Her sharp whisper came through trembling lips. "You're having a *daadi haus* added?" Why would her father add on separate rooms, where an older generation moves to live when the younger generation takes over the main house, when their household only contained him and her brother Jacob and now herself and Caleb?

Though she barely heard her *daed*'s response through her ringing ears, the blush that rose above his graying beard was obvious. "*Ach*, I figured Jacob might want to be marrying soon." The red deepened when he cleared his throat and continued sheepishly. "And I've been seeing a widow lately. So I might be…ah…doing that as well. I figured two new wives in a household might be one too many."

Lydia's head spun. Wary of the weakness in her knees, she leaned back against the buggy, grateful to find the support of the steel-wrapped wheel under her elbow and the wooden spokes pressed against her hip. If that was one too many, where would a returning single daughter fit in? If she even did? Absorbing her tension, Caleb's little chest expanded on an inhalation and he revived his volume. The harness jangled as the gelding backed up a step, tugging at the reins Henry held.

"Time we got the little one home," Henry mumbled as, escaping with alacrity, he led the horse to the shafts and began hitching him to the buggy.

Bouncing Caleb gently in her arms, she reluctantly met Jonah's gaze.

"I wouldn't have taken the job if I'd known you were coming back." Even with Caleb's sobs in her ear, Jonah's low voice cut through her.

She winced. Well, that put her in her place. It was her fault though. She'd done a good job of ensuring he'd felt that way before she'd left. *Leave them before they leave you.*

"I wouldn't have come back if I'd known you'd taken the job." Nausea threatened the moment the words left her mouth. Or maybe the churning was from the tension headache growing at the back of her neck, augmented by Caleb's wails. But even if she could, she wouldn't take the words back. Better to keep him at arm's length. She'd come back to repair her reputation and relationships. Except this one. This one would best remain fractured.

A muscle flexed in his jaw. "Well, you can remedy that. Last time I heard, the bus goes both ways."

She widened her eyes to keep the burning

at their backs at bay. She didn't intend to go back. But, with him in the house, potentially along with two new wives, could she now stay? Tempted to join Caleb in his wailing, she instead straightened from the wheel. Unfortunately, *her* tears wouldn't be remedied with a meal, a nap and a comforting back rub. With an obvious detour around Jonah, she slid back the buggy's door to carefully set the boy on the seat. Keeping a hand on him, she climbed into the buggy before her shaky knees buckled completely.

Settling Caleb back on her lap, she glanced outside, fixing her attention on the volleyball wedged under the unmoving man's elbow. It was easier than meeting the eyes that'd once gazed at her much differently. "You've got a game to play."

His strong throat, darkened by hours spent working in the sun, bobbed. "It's a far sight better than the ones you played." Pivoting on his heel, he strode away from the buggy, giving Henry a curt nod as he passed.

Lydia dashed away a few rogue tears before the buggy creaked as her *daed* climbed inside. Caleb's wailing subsided into squeaks and blubbering over the hard biscuit she'd dug from a bag she'd brought for his needs. She didn't speak until the gelding's quick trot had taken them a half mile down the road.

"A *daadi haus*?" she echoed. Her homecoming, such as it was, wasn't much. But this was an unexpected—and unwelcomed—blow.

Henry rubbed the back of his neck. "I... want to get married again."

Lydia hissed in a breath. Why? Why would any man want to marry again after living with her mother? She didn't voice the question. It wasn't her place to discuss her parents' marriage. Her *daed* had never said a word about the relationship, even after her *mamm* passed away. Lydia had wondered how he could sustain his steady and pleasant demeanor, even as she'd come to rely on it. But, barring meals, most of every waking moment he and her older *breider* had been out of the house. An escape not possible for her and her two sisters.

Lydia had thought her home, empty now of every female presence but herself, would be a haven. Her father's concern had been an accurate one. As the youngest son, her brother Jacob would eventually inherit the farm. If he was planning to wed, it would eventually be his wife's realm. And if her *daed* married... Two, much less three, women trying to run a household seldom worked. Especially if whomever Jacob or, *oh help*, her father was courting was someone Lydia had previously affronted in her...in her past life. Lydia pushed a swallow past the ache at the back of her throat. Since her targets, particularly the young ones, had been multiple, it was an unfortunate possibility.

If her own mother could only find fault with her, why would a stepmother, unrelated by blood, be any different? The sanctuary she'd planned to return home to suddenly looked like anything other than a refuge. Where would she and Caleb fit into the new household? What if the widow had children to be added into the family? Grown children? More who she might've offended moving into the house. Lydia wearily closed her eyes. The chickens were definitely coming home to roost.

Thankfully, Caleb had ceased his crying. Worn out from his bout of tears and lulled by the buggy's motion, he'd dropped to sleep against her shoulder. With a sigh, Lydia opened her eyes to face the road ahead. Whatever it might be.

"Do I know her?"

In her peripheral vision, she could see her *daed* smile, as if even the thought of this woman brought him pleasure. "*Nee*, I don't think so. She's from another district. But you'll meet her soon."

Well, at least the woman probably hadn't been a subject of her gossip. Still, dread pooled in Lydia's stomach at the prospect of her father's new wife soon taking up residence. Maybe it was a *gut* thing about a *daadi haus*. In fact, the faster it went up, the better. She didn't have any problems with it being built. Only with the builder.

"When will the addition be completed?" Perhaps, even now, he was wrapping up the finishing touches.

"*Ach*, not for a while yet. Jonah had to work around helping his *daed* with harvest. He recently finished shelling the outside of the addition and moved inside. So it'll be a few months yet before it's complete."

Lydia's shoulders drooped. When had Jonah focused his attention on carpentry? She remembered—her lips twisted, she remembered everything about him—that once his younger *breider* left school to help his *daed* in the dairy, Jonah had begun working with a local carpenter. But before she'd left, it'd only been part-time, and he hadn't been on his own.

"Why him?"

Her *daed* looked over in surprise. "Why

not? He's a *gut* man. It'd be hard to find a much more disciplined one in the community. He's a hard worker. Gaining quite a reputation for his carpentry work. I'm glad to have obtained his services before he was committed to other projects. With many Amish crews keeping busy doing work for the *Englisch*, it can be a wait if the job isn't an emergency or isn't a community project."

As they approached their farmstead, Lydia studied the new shape of their house, one she hadn't noted when, exhausted, she'd arrived in the dark last evening laden with Caleb and a few bags. She'd entered the house through the dimly lit mudroom. When she'd exited by way of the porch this morning, she'd been anxious about her uncertain reception at church and hadn't looked back at the house once she'd climbed into the buggy.

She sighed. The addition fit seamlessly into the existing structure. Lydia wasn't surprised. Jonah did everything well. He had prospects. He had good standing in the community. Jonah Lapp never did anything wrong. Except get tangled up with her.

Lydia slid the bread pans to the back of the counter and draped a clean dish towel over them. Dusting the flour from her hands, she looked toward the floor at the clanging that erupted from there.

"Are you going to bake too? Or are you just making more things for me to wash up?" She squatted in front of Caleb, who was happily banging away at cake pans he'd dragged from the cupboard. At her words, he grinned and patted on the metal bottoms again. She was glad his current entertainment allowed her to get some work done in the kitchen. As he now crawled at lightning speed, as long as he was making noise, she could keep track of his location without keeping both eyes, and generally one hand, on him.

Rising, Lydia opened a drawer and handed him a wooden spoon. "Here you go. Bang away. I'd much rather hear you than someone else." Moving to the sink to run water for dishes, Lydia frowned as she looked out the window. The "someone else" had arrived a little after sunrise. Her stomach had clenched when a buggy had turned into the lane while she was finishing feeding Caleb his breakfast. When Jonah emerged from it and scowled in the direction of the kitchen, she'd ducked away from the window, clenching the edge of the counter until her fingers turned white. She remained braced there while Caleb chattered from the high chair until it became obvious that, while Jonah had entered into the mudroom, now the connection between the two homes, he wasn't coming this way, instead had gone straight to the shell of the *daadi haus*.

Once they'd arrived home from church yesterday, she'd put the still sleeping Caleb down for a nap. She'd hesitantly entered the addition, the pine smell of new lumber wafting to her as soon as she stepped through the rough-cut door. Though all tools and the building supplies on hand were neatly organized and out of the way, she'd walked slowly over the subflooring, the lead in her stomach multiplying with every framed-in room she passed. As her *daed* had said, there was much work left to be done. Much work that meant the builder would be here for a long, long time. How was she to avoid him when he'd be only a wall or two away?

So far today, only occasional muted sounds emanated from the expanded area of the house. Still, Lydia slid out the drawer again and handed Caleb another spoon. She did dishes and cleaned the kitchen to the accompaniment of his one-man recital, her heart still thudding with an extra beat whenever sounds radiated from the central mudroom; the person generating them only a thin door and what she'd discovered to be a fickle door handle between them.

At the clatter of hooves, she glanced out the open kitchen window as a buggy came up the lane. Her brow furrowed. Who would be visiting? A farmer friend of her *daed* would, like him, be working in the field. Her *bruder*, Jacob, shouldn't be home until he finished for the day at his furniture-making job in town. She lifted a brow. Though yesterday had gone better than she'd expected, it was seriously doubtful any of the district's women would be coming over to welcome her back.

When the arrivals descended from the buggy, Lydia shot a glance to ensure Caleb was currently entertained before slipping into the common room to open the front door. Her older sister strode across the yard. Trailing behind were Lydia's two nieces. She smiled at their approach. She was glad to see Lucetta and the girls. They were family. But though she and her sister shared a history, she didn't know if they were really friends. Growing up in their home hadn't been an environment to nurture friendships. While she'd cringed in commiseration when their *mamm*'s displeasure was directed at her sisters, it was preferable to when turned toward her. Homesick, she'd written Lucetta after she'd left, but having never received anything in return, her correspondence had trickled to nothing.

"*Guder mariye*," she greeted them as they crossed the porch.

"Morning to you too." With a brief nod toward Lydia, Lucetta headed for the kitchen. The little girls, eyeing Lydia warily, hastily slipped through the door she held open. Lydia smiled at their backs as they scurried into the kitchen. They probably didn't remember her after her year of absence. Malinda had only been three and Fannie just a yearling when she'd left.

When she entered the kitchen, she saw the girls had joined Caleb with his pans. But instead of banging on them with the spoons the boy willingly shared, they cast guarded glances at their *mamm*.

Ignoring her children, Lucetta pulled out a chair and sat down at the table. "I could use some *kaffi*."

After snagging another wooden spoon and some dish towels from a drawer to drop in front of the trio, Lydia prepared coffee as requested. Turning from the counter, she glanced at the trio on the floor. Malinda had folded the towels, albeit unevenly, and the children were patting the new soft percussion with the spoons. Lydia smiled at them encouragingly although inwardly she winced at their careful movements.

"I saw you hiding out in the kitchen yesterday. Or were you doing penance for all the Sundays you skipped out on doing any tasks? I'm surprised they let you into their pristine ranks."

Lydia hunched a shoulder at Lucetta's observation. Yesterday hadn't been so bad. No one had been rude to her face. Some had even been quite kind. "It's been better than I'd hoped. Or at least it has so far." She set a cup down in front of her sister. "Perhaps our father has preached a sermon recently on 'Judge not, that ye be not judged.'"

Lucetta snorted. "I doubt that would stop me from being the main subject of disapproval. Or at least I was until you came back." After picking up her coffee, she took a sip. "I don't suppose you have anything to go with this."

"*Nee.* I haven't had time to make anything yet other than bread." Lydia lunged up from the seat she'd just settled into, troubled but not surprised of what the district's opinion was of her. She drew in a long breath. It was what she'd come back to face, after all. "I have some crackers that I'd brought for Caleb though, if you'd like."

Her sister wrinkled her nose at the offering. *"Nee."* She glanced over to where Fannie, her younger daughter, had left the other children and was twisting the doorknob to the mudroom. Brows lowering, Lucetta barked, "Leave that alone." Ducking her head, the little girl scooted the few feet back to where the other two were playing.

Opening a package of crackers, Lydia then pulled out three for the children. Caleb glommed on to his, but the girls took theirs with rounded eyes and hesitant fingers. Retrieving another three crackers, Lydia distributed those as well, earning shy smiles.

The kitchen chair creaked as Lucetta leaned back. Lydia wiped up a few cracker crumbs on the counter. Surely there should be something to say after a year's absence between sisters? But any closeness they might've had while in the same household had waned when Lucetta had married young and moved out, with Malinda arriving not much later.

Clearing her throat, she spoke into the uncomfortable silence. "Do you hear from Hadassah?"

Lucetta shook her head. "Not since she married that boy from another district and moved over."

Their mother hadn't been as hard on their youngest sister. Lydia had tried to protect her, stepping into frays directed at Hadassah, drawing their *mamm*'s censure instead. She hoped Hadassah, wed some months after Lydia had left for Pennsylvania, was doing better in her relationship than her older sister was. She hadn't known Hadassah's new husband well. Hadassah hadn't brought him around much before she'd left. Probably afraid Lydia would've flirted with him if she had. And she probably would've been right. Coffee, Lydia's stomach's sole content, churned there at the thought.

"Did Cousin Mary kick you out or something? Is that why you're back?"

"Nee." Dipping her chin, Lydia stared at the worn linoleum. Though Mary supported her return, she would've let Lydia stay with her in Pennsylvania. But Lydia felt it was best for both women if she left her cousin's home.

Lucetta poured sugar into her coffee. "I never understood why you brought the boy with you instead of having him stay with Mary. Didn't she want to keep him? As her daughter's child, he's her only living descendent now, isn't he?"

Shuddering at the scrape of the spoon against the crockery, Lydia edged over to stand between her sister and Caleb. "Cousin Mary is getting older. She wasn't sure that she'd be able to keep up with a little one by herself." She folded her arms over her chest. "I'm glad to have him."

"A baby will slow you down from getting out to meet people."

"I don't plan to do much socializing."

"That'll be a switch for you. I can help you out if you change your mind. I've found some fun parties." Lucetta waggled her eyebrows. Brows—to Lydia's narrowed gaze—that looked suspiciously plucked.

"How and why are you finding parties?"

Her sister shrugged a slender shoulder. "As to why, shifting from one household to another wasn't the escape I was hoping for. It's still a drudgery, just without our *mamm*'s continual carping. And as for how…" Lucetta's lips tilted into a smirk. "I haven't lost my touch for sneaking out."

Lydia's wide gaze darted to the children playing quietly nearby. She lowered her voice. "You're sneaking out at night? What about the girls?"

"Oh, Peter is in the *daadi haus*. He'll hear them if they wake up and there's an issue."

Lydia pressed her hands against her cheeks. She couldn't imagine leaving children in the house at night, even with someone staying in the extended structure.

"But you're married! You're baptized!" Although their home, filled with their mother's rampant criticism, hadn't been the happiest, Lydia had always known she wanted to stay in Amish life, making the decision to be baptized well before she'd left for Pennsylvania. Granted, she'd failed in some of her vows, had made her own mistakes. Mistakes she was trying to rectify. Mistakes for which she knew there'd someday be a reckoning.

"I wouldn't have gotten baptized if I hadn't needed to in order to marry. Maybe I should've left before I did. I was just trying to get out of the house any way I could. I know you were doing the same. Just with more effort and less success." The smirk had yet to leave Lucetta's face. It struck Lydia that the expressions of her sister's that she'd striven to emulate when she was younger were particularly unattractive when one was the recipient. *Gut* thing she no longer intended to model them.

"The gatherings are mainly *Englisch,* but occasionally a few Amish attend. I think I've even seen the district's schoolteacher there. Why don't you join me?"

Chapter Three

Jonah froze at the click of the doorknob. The insulation's kraft paper backing crackled under his fingers as he turned toward the kitchen. Was Lydia coming in? His heart rate doubled as he watched the door. When it never opened beyond a slender sliver, he blew out a breath and straightened, gripping a roll of insulation in each hand.

At the sound of female voices, *her* voice, he paused. Recalling their bitter conversation yesterday, his stomach churned, much as it'd done since he'd spoken to her. Should he apologize? He took a step toward the door. He'd been the one to start with harsh words. Start and continue. Hurt people hurt people, his *mamm* would say. He hadn't paid much mind to the adage until now. But the saying was true.

He'd been hurt. His chest expanded on a deep inhalation. He'd *let* himself be hurt. There was a difference. Jonah scowled. And he'd wanted to hurt her in return. Was it the pride he wasn't supposed to have in their culture? He surely wasn't the first and he probably wouldn't be the last to watch her go from his arms straight to another's. The others had just shrugged, but he was the only one wearing the willow over her moving, albeit quickly, on. Fool that he was, he'd…cared. Even more foolish, he'd thought she had as well.

Ach. The more he pouted over his unrequited love, the more likely she'd realize the reason for his bitterness and mock him for it. If he didn't want her to know he was still hurting from her rejection, he needed to act like he wasn't.

Turning toward the addition, he hesitated at a question that slipped through the door. Why *had* she come back? Though he held his breath, Lydia never answered, or responded so softly he couldn't hear, unlike her staunch defense for keeping the boy. He could see yesterday that she took *gut* care of the child.

His feet stayed rooted on the mudroom's concrete floor as he listened to the muted conversation. He raised an eyebrow at the news she didn't plan to socialize. The Lydia who'd left couldn't get enough of it. His mouth tightened over the snippets of their home life. He'd always wondered. Henry Troyer was a *gut* fellow, an easygoing man. Their *mamm*, though Jonah had only seen her at church and other general community functions, had always looked to him as if she'd just taken a sip of milk that'd already turned sour. Maybe it was life that had appeared sour to her. Hurt people hurt people.

Had he been part of Lydia's attempt to get out of the house? His stomach roiled further, as if he was the one who'd drunk sour milk. Had he been used? Had her affection only been an attempt to hook a husband? If that'd been her game, it hadn't worked out the way she'd hoped. Jonah's lips tipped into a humorless smile. Though it would've if she hadn't played it with someone else quite so fast. *Ja*, he would've asked her to marry him. Again, more fool he.

Still, it disturbed him that Lydia's household was such that the girls had been so desperate to leave. Even now, he felt a twinge of inclination to comfort her, one he quickly stifled at Lucetta's invitation to Lydia to join her at parties.

Renewing his grip on the insulation, Jonah

winced when he heard the schoolteacher mentioned as he strode toward the door to the addition. He liked Grace Kauffman well enough. She was doing a *gut* job with the district's children. A factor in a teacher's selection though was their embrace of Amish values. Some of the men on the school board wouldn't be happy to hear Lucetta's comment. If it was true she was attending *Englisch* parties, surely Grace would change her behavior before she got into trouble. If it was false, hopefully the rumor would cease before it did the young woman damage. Jonah grimaced as he set the insulation on the plywood subflooring in the bedroom. Before she'd left, Lydia's reputation as a gossiper had eclipsed her sister's.

Unfurling a roll, he measured what he needed, wielding his utility knife with decisive slices as he sectioned off pieces. He hadn't wanted to hear Lydia's response to Lucetta's invitation. Well, he'd wanted to hear it, but he was afraid of what it might be. She'd said earlier she didn't plan to socialize. Did that mean no parties?

Though he'd never gone, he'd known several Amish youth who'd attended them. Even during *rumspringa* when a youth was exploring aspects of the world outside their Amish community and seeking a mate, he hadn't been interested in that type of entertainment. Not in drinking. Not in the loud music, nor cars. Not in carrying a phone or dressing in non-Amish clothes. He'd quickly determined to be baptized and join the church, where rules forgiven for those who were not yet members had consequences for those who were.

His weakness hadn't been the parties or other things. It'd been his interest in Lydia.

Her interest had been every male, single or sometimes not, in the district. Still, it'd taken him months after she'd left before he seriously looked at other girls. And then, it'd been one who'd been looking at him first. Securing the insulation in between the studs in rapid sequence, Jonah snorted. He must have a type. Either he didn't like to chase, or he had a thing for girls who were a bit forward. But though she obviously was interested in male company, Rebecca Mast was nowhere near the flirt Lydia was. It didn't matter to him. He wasn't going to break the rules of the *Ordnung* again. After the guilt and heartache of doing so with Lydia, breaking rules was something he'd never repeat.

Lydia was exhausted from the strain of her sister's company by the time she watched

Lucetta and the girls climb into the buggy and wave farewell as they headed down the lane. A bit of tension had dissipated though, tempered by a small sense of achievement, when both girls had smiled shyly and waved as they'd scampered across the porch. They'd reminded her of when she'd been young with her sisters. They hadn't talked much either. At least not until they discovered attention wasn't always negative, like they'd received from their *mamm*. Attention from boys could be very positive, and from girls who'd avidly listen to tales as long as they were about others and not their audience.

She didn't know the current schoolteacher. The young woman had arrived in the area after Lydia had left. As for herself attending any parties—those kinds of parties—she had no interest in that anymore, if she'd ever really had at the time she'd been going to them. It'd just been a way out of the house, a way of balancing negative attention of the day with positive notice in the dark. After a while, for the persona she'd created, it was almost expected she'd attend.

Lucetta had scowled when Lydia had flatly refused to leave Caleb. Grossly uncomfortable at discussing the particular topic in front of the girls, Lydia had been relieved when the conversation moved on to other things, though she'd responded with a noncommittal *hmm* when her sister had brought up more gossip. Closing the front door to the trio, she sighed. She didn't want the girls to experience the childhood they'd had, where everything had been met with their mother's disapproval at best or harsh criticism as the norm.

What she was seeing in Lucetta provoked memories of growing up with her *mamm*. It was like holding up a mirror. She shared Lucetta's genetics. Her environment. Her history. Lydia twisted her fingers together. And with all that, more than likely, her future. Lydia's breath escaped in a long exhale. This was why she'd never tie herself to anyone she cared for. It would sentence the man to a life of unhappiness. There was a flip side to Happy Wife, Happy Life—Bitter Wife, Miserable Life. And she couldn't do that to Jon— she caught herself—to a worthy man.

The little girls hadn't talked much today, at least not to her. She pushed up a smile. They'd certainly chattered with Caleb though, and he with them. So much so that maybe he was all talked out, as the kitchen was now quiet. Stepping back into it, she glanced to where she'd left him playing with colorful blocks she'd earlier retrieved for the children.

With a sharp inhalation, her gaze swept the room. The empty room. Her heart stuttered when she noticed the partially open door to the mudroom. Rushing across the kitchen, she flung it open. With a quick brace of both hands on the doorjamb, she caught herself before she collided with Jonah, who held a contented Caleb in his arms.

Jonah stapled the measured piece of insulation between the wall studs and bent to get another. He was working on what would be the outer wall of the bedroom. He'd needed to start somewhere and that was the farthest part of the addition from the central mudroom and the woman in the kitchen beyond it. Every time he stepped into the mudroom to retrieve another roll of insulation, he refrained from pausing to listen to the voices coming through the fractionally opened door.

Though dwelling on the parts of the conversation he had heard at least kept him from brooding on the argument—the latest—he'd had with his *daed* as they'd wrapped up milking this morning. Jonah's hand flexed on the stapler, shooting an extra staple in between the studs. Except his *daed*, Zebulun Lapp, didn't argue. One could tell he was listening from his rare and frequently insightful questions. But though his *daed* would maintain a bland expression, tilt his head in consideration, even nod at the end of the dialogue, he'd still proceed exactly as he'd done before.

Although, Jonah sighed, he had to admit his father *had* brought home the fly-trapping ribbon earlier this summer a few days after they'd discussed it. Instructing his sons to string it around the barn and milk parlor, it'd cut down on the fly population that bothered man and beast. And, while Zebulun still used a battery lantern himself, he'd purchased LED headlights for the boys for when they'd head out before sunrise to milk in a dark barn.

But there were so many other things, at least to Jonah's mind, that could improve the efficiency of their operation. Some things were already allowed by the *Ordnung*. Others were, well, not specifically disallowed. And with adoption by other members in the district, might become fully accepted. If only his *daed* could be convinced to change.

Jonah scowled when he discovered he'd cut a section a full foot short. He didn't usually make mistakes. Which was a *gut* thing, as he despised making them. His perfectionism was one of the reasons he was getting a solid reputation as a carpenter. While he'd balanced apprenticing under an uncle while farming with his *daed*, he'd set out on his own in the past year. Now he was busy enough that he left for his job as soon as morning milking was completed and didn't get home much before evening chores. Chores and milking which could be done faster and more efficiently if his *daed* would listen and incorporate some of his suggestions.

Though the farm wasn't going to be his—it would go to his youngest *bruder*, as was the custom—Jonah still wanted to see it do as well as possible. There were ways of doing things that'd make it more profitable than it was now.

And he liked farming. He liked working with his *daed*. As the oldest son, he'd always been his father's first help when his mother was busy with the younger children. They'd increased the herd size when he'd finished school after eighth grade. He loved the comradery with his *breider* on the family operation. He just didn't know if there was room anymore for all of them.

He cut a short section to repair his mistake. Better for now that he just kept his head on carpentry and not on farming or the woman on the other side of the mudroom's door.

Unrolling another bale of insulation, Jonah double-checked his lengths before he cut this time. At least in his carpentry work, he could make his own decisions, could improve efficiencies where he found them, as long as it met the needs of the customer, of course. Could walk away at the end of the day having viewed obvious progress. With the strips precut, he rapidly applied the last of them to the wall. As there weren't any gas lines to run through the walls, something done in more progressive Amish settlements for lighting, the work went much faster.

Having finished with the insulation, Jonah's footsteps echoed through the hollow construction area as he went to gather materials for his next task. Stepping through the door to the mudroom, he jerked to a halt.

"Hey, buddy, that's probably not a very steady support you've got there."

The toddler turned to look at him from where he'd pulled up on a stack of framing studs. Standing on wavering legs, he regarded Jonah with wide eyes. Moving slowly so as to not scare the boy, Jonah crossed the concrete floor and squatted to the little one's level. The boy drew back, releasing his hold on the lumber to sit, with a practiced plop, on his padded bottom.

"*Ja.* I think that's a *gut* idea. Those boards can be pretty wobbly. How did you get in here, anyway?" The boy looked back toward the door to the kitchen, open just wide enough for someone his size to slip through.

"Outnumbered by the women folk and determined to escape, huh. *Ach*, I guess I can't blame a fellow for that. But if they haven't missed you yet, they will soon. Your…" what was Lydia to the boy anyway, a cousin? "Well anyway, I'm sure she'll be wondering where you are, as she seemed pretty attentive to you yesterday." Glad he'd had some practice as an uncle, Jonah slipped his hands under the boy's arms, gripping the sturdy chest, and lifted the toddler to rest against his shoulder.

"You're a *gut* deal quieter than when I met you yesterday. Glad to know you have a different attitude and more than one volume, since it looks like you'll be my neighbor of sorts for a while." The boy studied him solemnly before reaching out to touch Jonah's beardless check.

"*Ja.* I don't have the beard that Henry has. That's because he was married several years ago and I'm not." Jonah glanced at the door and dropped his voice, "Though I might've been if someone was who I thought she was. *Gut* thing I found out she wasn't before I put myself in a position to grow a beard, huh."

Jonah gave the little one an experimental bounce. An experiment that seemed to be successful as the boy giggled. "I suppose since you've shown you can adjust your attitude, I'll have to follow your example and adjust mine as well. Do you think she will too, as we're doing ours? I don't… I don't want her to see that she bothers me. You might not know it, but we have a history. Though, while she was a chapter in mine, I was more like a mere sentence in hers."

The little one furrowed his brows as if in sympathy. Jonah grinned. "*Ja.* I know. It was humbling. But this is something we can discuss later, if I see you around. Right now, there's someplace you should be and it's not here amongst my construction tools and supplies."

Crossing the concrete floor, he stopped in front of the kitchen door and raised a hand to rap on the jamb. Before he could, the door swung wide to reveal the one who'd plagued his thoughts. Lydia's eyes were wide in her pale face. She blanched even further at the sight of him.

Jonah hastened to reassure her. "He's all right. The door was partway open and he slipped through."

Lydia wanted to snatch Caleb from where he was comfortably ensconced against Jonah's muscular shoulder a short, disturbing foot away. Instead, she drew in careful breaths. She was overreacting. He would see it. *Calm down.* Thankfully, upon spying her, Caleb leaned in her direction and reached out his arms. Lydia didn't know what she would've done if he hadn't. Eagerly, she reached in return. When she brushed Jonah's hands in the exchange, her heart rate galloped. Once Caleb was in her arms, she retreated a step into the kitchen. Only then did her pulse begin the descent toward normalcy.

Jonah regarded her a moment, his green eyes pensive. He cleared his throat. "He's a little young to be an apprentice. Maybe in a few years."

Lydia's breath shallowed at the prospect. *It would break my heart to have him work with you.* She cleared her throat as well. "I'm sorry he bothered you."

"He was no bother. I didn't expect a baby to come crawling in. Just a surprise."

You have no idea. "Well, thanks for keeping him out of trouble."

Jonah opened his mouth like he was going to say something else. Closing it, he drew in a breath through his nose. His lips twitched when Caleb patted her on the mouth.

"He's solid. I didn't expect him to be

so stout when I picked him up. What's his name?"

Automatically catching the baby's hand, Lydia placed a kiss on the palm and pulled it away from her face. "Caleb."

Jonah furrowed his brow. "Is that how you're related to the Pennsylvania cousins?"

She lowered her own. "What?"

"The ones you stayed with. Are you related through your grandfather? Didn't you have one named Caleb?"

Lydia retreated another step. Her *grossdaadi* Caleb had been her favorite relative. When had she told Jonah? And why had he remembered? "*Nee*. That's not how we're related." Withdrawing an additional step, Lydia moved to shut the door. She paused at Jonah's grimace.

"Listen…" He rubbed a hand over the back of his neck. "I don't like this situation any more than you do. But I committed to this job, and when I make a commitment, I keep it. So I'm going to be here. I'll stay out of your way as much as possible. But we're going to run into each other. We might as well…make some kind of peace with that."

She hissed in a breath. Maybe it was better this way. Like building immunity to something by repeated exposures. She dipped her chin in acknowledgment. "*Ja.* It's too small of a community to try to avoid each other." Forcing a smile, she quipped, "And while you're making it bigger, it's an even smaller house." When Caleb squirmed, leaning toward the man before her, Lydia shifted the boy to bounce him on her other hip. "I'll do a better job of keeping him out of your way though."

Jonah gave a slow nod. "He's a grand boy. But that might be a *gut* idea, with all the tools and supplies and such where I'm working. Don't want anyone to get hurt."

Lydia shook her head. "*Nee,* we wouldn't want that." Jonah's gaze followed her as she shut the door, the *click* sounding overly loud in the quiet kitchen. Resting her cheek against Caleb's downy head, she sagged against the door and considered the man on the other side of it. Too late. That caution had come a little too late. Hurting was what she did to the people in her life.

Chapter Four

❧

Lydia had done dishes so often she could do them without looking. Good thing, as, rather than watching her dishcloth swishing over the plates and cups in the sudsy water, she was looking out the open window to where Jonah sat under a maple tree, eating a sandwich he'd brought with him for lunch.

Now that she was here, she'd be expected to prepare a noon meal for her *daed* or anyone else working on the place, conventional hospitality reciprocated throughout the community. Lydia knew, whether it was taken out to the field or the men came to the house, that lunch would be provided where Henry was working today. She felt a twinge of guilt for not doing so for Jonah.

He hadn't asked. She hadn't offered. Her *daed* hadn't been around to notice. Yet.

Could she face Jonah across the table? With Caleb in a high chair nearby? A few days ago, her shoulders would've locked in hunched unison at the prospect. But after their brief, albeit stilted conversation yesterday, though they hadn't interacted since and Lydia ensured the kitchen door to the mudroom remained shut, she no longer tensed at every sound that came from the *daadi haus*. In fact, it was somewhat comforting that someone was on the property, even though it was someone who...unsettled her. It could be fine; it *would* be fine. As long as he stayed on the other side of the door.

The maple tree was still as green as the grass on which Jonah sat, though several leaves appeared dipped in the scarlet that would adorn the full tree in a few more weeks. Jonah faced the lane, allowing Lydia the opportunity to look her fill at him, something she hadn't been able to do since she'd returned, or allowed herself to do for even longer. He was leaning back on one elbow, his long legs stretched in front of him. An indentation circling his thick hair showed where his now absent straw hat had been pressed on his head. A breeze lifted a few of the freed dark curls. Lydia smiled. He'd always despised those curls, claiming he looked like a hedgehog whenever he removed his hat.

She'd always loved them. She'd wished she'd had the right to brush them from his forehead when, like now, the curls were so long, they surely dipped over his eyebrows.

She turned from the window. But she never would. Or at least, never would again.

"It'll be a bit of time before your hair is long enough to trim." She rescued what remained of a banana from Caleb's grip and began cleaning him and the tray from the residue of his meal. The clatter of hooves coming up the driveway sounded through the window. Lydia's stomach clenched. Was it Lucetta again? She'd enjoyed the time since her sister had left, giving the house a thorough cleaning before catching up on laundry and then sewing new clothes for Caleb. Except for awareness of Jonah on the other side of the closed door, it'd been peaceful. She wasn't ready for more of her sister's drama. But other than Lucetta, it wasn't like she'd left any other friends who might come visiting.

But it could be someone looking for her *daed*. Freeing Caleb from the high chair, Lydia peered out to see who the arrival was. She frowned when Rebecca Mast descended from the buggy to secure her horse to the hitch post. Lydia's stomach knotted when the girl rushed over to Jonah, who'd risen at her arrival. What had she expected? She'd made sure she'd burned any interest he may have had in her. No surprise he'd moved on to someone more worthy. And Rebecca's family was far more worthy. Rebecca's older sister Rachel had been a prominent victim of Lydia's venomous gossip. A target, Lydia now understood, born of jealousy and envy. When Rebecca reached out to grasp Jonah's hand, Lydia fisted her own. Another target due to jealousy and envy. *If* she let it be. Uncurling her fingers one by one, she swiped them down the front of her apron. Something she'd vowed never to let happen again. Never again since…

The backs of her eyes burned as she tenderly wiped a missed smudge from Caleb's cheek. "With *Gott's* help I'll try. Sometimes things seem too hard to do on your own." She tapped him on the nose with a gentle finger. "But I'm not on my own. I have you. And you have me. That might not seem like much, but I'm better than I was." Knuckling away an escaping tear, she amended, "At least I'm trying to be. Especially for you."

Caleb twisted toward the window at the unexpected sound that drifted through. Lydia cocked her head in the direction as well. Was that…crying? Looking out the window, she saw Jonah awkwardly patting Rebecca's shoulder as the young woman buried her face in her hands. What on earth had happened? Was someone hurt? Had someone died? Lydia was frozen for an instant at the memory of another time, another's grief. A moment later, she was out the door.

The relief on Jonah's face was unmistakable as she, with Caleb on her hip, crossed the yard to where the couple huddled in the shade of the tree.

"Rebecca is frightened for her *mamm*." Although their hands were no longer entwined, Jonah continued to pat Rebecca's shoulder.

"Has there been an accident? Is Susannah hurt?" Lydia's breath came in pants at the flashbacks to another accident, this one not in the brightness of an autumn noon, but in the dark of night. Her knees threatened to buckle. Caleb squirmed as her arms clenched about him.

Lifting her head, Rebecca brushed tears from her cheeks. "No. No accident. She's… she's having a *boppeli*."

Lydia drew in a deep breath and consciously eased her grip on the wiggling baby. She'd always admired Susannah Mast, now Weaver.

Maybe it was one of the reasons she'd been envious of Rachel.

Though pregnancies and childbirth were seldom publicly discussed, they were a common occurrence in the Amish community, with their belief in the blessings of a large family. That didn't mean there wasn't an awareness of the potential danger of childbirth.

"Is she by herself? Do we need to contact the midwife?"

"Hannah is already with her." Hannah Bartel, Jonah's sister, was the community's midwife now that the older Mennonite woman who'd served in the role for decades was retiring.

"Then she is in *gut* care."

Though the young woman nodded, her chin trembled. "I just didn't know what to do there. How to not be in the way. I shouldn't be upset, it being such a normal thing. It's just…it's just that she's older now, and I know I shouldn't, because whatever happens is *Gott's* will, but I'm worried about her. And the *boppeli*. Some of my infant siblings…haven't survived before, so I'm afraid for this one." Rebecca's breath was released in shudders. "I know my *mamm* is as well, as I've overheard her speaking of it with Jethro." She burst into renewed tears.

* * *

Jonah blinked in surprise when, after Lydia's brief hesitation, he suddenly found himself with an armful of baby as she handed him the boy and pulled the sobbing girl into her embrace. The little one seemed equally startled. Leaning away from Jonah's chest, he studied him with a wrinkled brow over wary eyes. Jonah tried a few experimental bounces, which seemed to have worked for the boy before. Brow clearing, Caleb clapped his hands together.

"*Ja.* We've met briefly before, haven't we," he murmured to the boy. "We got along all right then, at least for a little while. I think we can now. Just, please don't start crying. I don't seem to do well with that." He couldn't recall Hannah or Gail, his two sisters, ever weeping like Rebecca was now doing. While they'd been seeing each other the past few months, Jonah wasn't sure what to do with the sobbing girl other than provide reassuring pats.

But Lydia had instinctively known. He glanced to where she, with an arm around Rebecca, was guiding the young woman up the steps and over to a porch swing that hung from the white painted ceiling. Settling Rebecca on the swing's wooden slats, she sat down beside her. Jonah, trailing in their wake, gave Caleb an extra bounce as he climbed each step, making the little one giggle.

"Even though she's older now, your *mamm* is a strong woman and no stranger to childbirth. She and Hannah will make a *gut* team. She and the babe are in *Gott's* hands, as we all are."

Rebecca dabbed her eyes with her apron at Lydia's encouraging words.

Lydia set the swing gently into motion. "I don't know much of your siblings, only vaguely remember that they were lost shortly after they were born. But if their issues were genetic, this one is a bit different. This child doesn't have the same father as they did."

Caleb kicked his feet against Jonah's chest. Stepping over to the porch swing, Jonah jingled the excess chain that extended from the hook securing the device to the ceiling. He lifted the boy up so he could reach and jingle it as well. Lydia looked over. Her breath snagged when she caught sight of them.

"He's all right. He's safe," Jonah assured her, keeping a secure grip on the boy's sturdy body.

With an uncertain nod, Lydia returned her attention to the woman beside her. After dashing a hand across her cheeks, Rebecca drew in a steadying breath. "Jethro is so excited, though he tries not to show it. Not that he doesn't care for Amos and me. But he never expected to have a child of his own."

Lydia's eyebrow rose. "Jethro generally seems so reserved. I can't imagine him volunteering that information in public."

Under her reddened nose, Rebecca's lips twitched. "Well, I overheard him and *Mamm* talking about that as well."

Lydia smiled. "You seem to be doing a lot of overhearing."

"I guess I have. Only I don't tell it all like you do."

Jonah almost lost his grip on the squirming baby at Rebecca's words. His gaze shot to her. She slapped a hand over her mouth and turned widened eyes to Lydia. Though her tear-flushed coloring had been receding while sitting on the swing, she was again as red as she'd been while sobbing.

Lydia drew in a breath. "That's fair." Her slender throat bobbed in a swallow. "And unfortunately true. Don't worry. I won't share any of this. Although I do understand your stepfather's excitement. A *boppeli* can bring an immeasurable sense of joy." She reached for Caleb, who was angling in her direction. Jonah let the boy go, his arms feeling oddly empty at the loss of the little one. To assuage the peculiar sensation, he crossed them over his chest.

"I'm s-sorry," Rebecca stammered.

"Why should you be sorry?" Caleb settled into Lydia's arms like maple syrup on a warm pancake. Using her foot, she kept the swing in motion. "As I said, it's true. I can't change the past." Silent for a moment, she cleared her throat before continuing. "Only strive to keep some things there."

She straightened the boy's pant leg, which had ridden up to his knee. "I trust that *Gott* will keep the issues your family has had in the past as well, and that your *mamm* and new sibling will be fine." A small smile touched her lips. "I remember when Caleb was born. The excitement, the fear, the uncertainty. But it is all worth it when your *boppeli* is set in your arms." Her jaw dropped slightly when she looked up to find Rebecca's and Jonah's attention on her. She shut her mouth with a click of teeth. "Or so I've heard."

Pushing off the swing, she rose to her feet. Jonah reached out to assist her with the boy, but she stepped around him, avoiding his outstretched hand. Reaching the door, she turned back to Rebecca. "I look forward to visiting your *mamm* and the new little one soon."

Rebecca stood as well. With a lowered

brow, she considered the red-haired woman. "You're not what I remembered."

Lydia gave a rueful smile. "I think that's probably a *gut* thing. Please let me know if you and your *mamm* need anything. Does she have someone coming in to help?"

"*Ja.* One of the younger Raber girls."

Even Jonah could sense the awkwardness that now threaded through the conversation. It wasn't long before Lydia said farewell and entered the house. Prior to her slipping through the door, Jonah was oddly moved by the solitary picture she made.

"I'm so embarrassed. I shouldn't have said that."

Drawing in a long breath, he turned back to see Rebecca press her hands against cheeks still rosy, either from her bout of tears or from the words she'd unintentionally spoken. He forced a nonchalant shrug as he accompanied her down the porch steps. "As she'd said, it was true. Lydia was quite a gossip before she left." Even though accurate, the words tasted bitter on his tongue.

Rebecca led the way to where her buggy was hitched. "After the rumors Lydia had spread about my sister, I didn't talk with her much, but I'd heard that when she went to Pennsylvania, she was going there to stay. I wonder what happened, now that she's come back with a little one after the loss of her cousin."

Jonah looked over his shoulder to see a shadow appear in the kitchen window. When Lydia had left last fall, he'd subtly sought news regarding her abrupt departure. He'd heard the same. That she wasn't returning. Even knowing it was for the best, he'd grieved until his *mamm* had questioned whether his reduced appetite and abnormal silences meant he was ill.

Nee. Just foolish, for longing for something that probably hadn't existed in the first place. He'd fallen for an illusion. Lydia hadn't been the girl he thought she was. Everyone else had been right and he'd been duped. At the touch on his arm, he dragged his attention back to Rebecca.

"Well, I suppose I should be sorry for coming to blubber all over you."

He smiled, knowing she expected it of him. "I'm none the worse for wear." *And it wasn't me who comforted your tears.* Stifling the urge to glance toward the kitchen window again, he instead gave Rebecca a hand up the step to her buggy. Her hand was nice, strong and slender in his. Jonah tried not to recall the jolt that'd raced through him when his hands had accidentally brushed Lydia's as they'd exchanged the baby the other day. *This* was where his attention needed to remain, this woman, these hands. He and Rebecca were well on their way to being a couple, after all.

"Please let me know how your family is doing. Or if I can do anything to help. Although, as she'd said," he tilted his head toward the house, "with Hannah taking care of her, your *mamm* is in *gut* hands."

For a moment, Rebecca's face clouded before she sniffed and picked up the reins. "I should get back. Hopefully the *boppeli* will arrive before I need to go in to work this evening. But I'll see you later this week?"

With a smile and a nod, Jonah went to untie her horse. Crossing the yard to the maple tree, he lifted his hand in farewell as the buggy rattled down the gravel lane. When he stooped to pick up the remains of his lunch, he scowled to discover enterprising ants had laid claim to the partially wrapped sandwich he'd left perched on top of a paper bag. With a sigh, he tore the rest of the sandwich into pieces to toss them over the yard for scavengers. Crumpling the trash, he headed inside to pitch it with other refuse that'd accumulated with the construction project. Stepping into the mudroom, Jonah hesitated in front of the door to the kitchen. He stared at the closed white portal. Firming his lips, he gave the door a quick rap, and turned the knob.

Chapter Five

Caleb looked up from the blocks he was playing with. Seeing the open door, he scampered on his hands and knees in that direction. Lydia scooped him up before he got halfway across the floor and set him on her hip as she eyed Jonah warily.

Under their dual regard, Jonah shifted his feet. "I just wanted to thank you for your help out there. With Rebecca crying and all. I wasn't sure what to do. How to respond." Jonah shrugged. "I guess I'm not very *gut* with tears."

Lydia drew in a long breath. "I'm sure she was just glad to be with you. Being around someone you…" Ducking her chin, she continued in a murmur, one low enough that Jonah barely made out the words. "…care for always makes you feel better when you're upset."

Jonah rubbed a hand over the back of his neck. He hadn't spoken to anyone in regard to the blow she'd dealt to his heart and pride. The prospect of doing so then—and now—seemed inconceivable. Did that mean he didn't want to acknowledge how much he'd hurt because that would reveal how much she'd meant to him? Or did that mean he didn't care for anyone enough to share his pain? His hurt? Or that even when hurt, his pride was too much to let himself be seen as vulnerable? Or a fool.

"*Ja.* Well, we've been walking out for a few months." Though Amish couples usually kept their relationships covert, some part of him wanted Lydia to know he was seeing someone. Wanted her to know that at least one woman preferred him over others. But if that was his intent, why did the admission, as soon as it'd escaped, bother him? He liked Rebecca. He respected her. He trusted her. Something he would never do again with Lydia.

Raising her head to reveal a rueful smile, Lydia nodded. "I wish you both the best."

They regarded each other across the silent kitchen. With a quiet sigh, Jonah reached to shut the door.

"Ba!"

Glancing back, he saw Caleb pointing at him. "Ba!" the little one insisted.

Jonah grinned. "We need to get you out about a farm a bit more. You've got the wrong species. I'm not a sheep."

"I don't know, your hair's looking a bit woolly." Lydia's lips quirked into a slight smile.

Lifting his hat a fraction from his head, Jonah swept a hasty hand through the rioting curls before jerking the brim back down. "Maybe the sheep have the right idea. I suppose I'm about due for a shearing."

Lydia tucked an escaped strand of hair behind her ear. "I…uh…saw you pitch your sandwich into the yard. What happened?"

He grimaced. "Enough ants had discovered it that I relinquished the meal to their higher numbers."

Though she winced in empathy, her slight smile grew to a full-blown one. For a moment, Jonah caught his breath. It was like watching a rosebud unfurl.

"Are you still hungry? I could make you another… If you'd like."

He slowly nodded, his heart thumping more than it should at the smile and the look in her blue eyes. It wasn't the come hither smile she'd perfected and used with more success than he wanted to remember on the young men of Miller's Creek. That was never the smile that'd attracted him. This one was sincere, a little shy. Like the Lydia he thought he'd once known. Honest. Although that was a word he'd had trouble equating with her after she'd used him. But this look, this smile. Why did it feel like he was trying to gain the trust of a creature that'd lost confidence in itself because of prior bad handling?

"I think I'd like."

With a small nod, she gestured toward the kitchen table. "If you want to have a seat, I'll take care of it. Ham or roast beef?" Setting Caleb down on the floor, she moved to the refrigerator.

"Roast beef. With mayo if you have it." He sat. To his delight, after a brief hesitation, Caleb crawled over. Using Jonah's pants leg, he pulled himself up to stand. Apparently quite pleased with his feat, he grinned and patted Jonah's knee.

Lydia almost dropped the jar of mayonnaise when she turned from the refrigerator and saw them together. "If he's a bother…"

"*Nee.* Not at all. I'm comfortable around little ones. I have younger brothers. Now that my sisters have made me an uncle, I've had even more practice lately. I'm not going to break him. And you handed him to me before, remember? We got along just fine."

"*Ja*, well, I wasn't thinking then. I was just reacting."

Jonah was glad she'd turned away to make the sandwiches and didn't see his frown. *The way you reacted when you raced from my arms to another man's? Were you thinking then? Thinking about how much you hurt me?* When she turned around to hand him a plate with a large sandwich neatly cut from corner to corner, he made sure a smile was pasted on his face.

"*Denki.*" Taking a bite, he nodded in appreciation. "I think between me and the ants, I got the better deal. This sandwich is much improved over the one I'd brought."

Her cheeks grew rosy. Jonah took another bite and wiped his mouth with the paper napkin she'd handed him along with the plate, relieved that he could do so without any signs of the trembling he felt. How could a woman who'd been as free as she had with other men blush at a mild compliment? The paradox she'd presented had been one of the things that'd attracted him in the first place. Overly confident, even aggressive on some occasions, timid on others. He'd always liked a puzzle. But she was one he didn't think he'd ever be able to solve.

"I suppose I could get you a cookie or two as well if you're still hungry."

He grunted. "I have to compete at mealtimes with three younger brothers. I'm always hungry."

Three cookies immediately appeared on his plate. He picked one out. Caleb, still standing at his knee, pointed. "Mamamama."

"I'm assuming you're not saying *mamm* but just asking me for a bite." He looked over at Lydia, who stared at them with rounded eyes. Jonah furrowed his brows. "It's all right, isn't it? I won't give him one if you don't want me to."

"Ah…*nee*. It's fine. I just…um…he makes new sounds all the time."

"And probably will from here on out. Before you know it, it will be an emphatic *no*." Breaking off a toddler-size chunk from the cookie, he handed it to the boy, smiling when Caleb started gnawing on it without hesitation. "You're right. She's a *gut* cook."

"*Daed* mentioned he'll be finishing up where he's helping out soon and I'll need to fix him meals when he's home. I suppose, if you're interested, I could feed you as well since I'll be cooking anyway."

He glanced up from watching the boy. She

was looking not at him, but at the glass of tea she'd just filled.

"That'd...that'd be nice. I'd appreciate it."

Lydia hunched a shoulder. "It's no more than my *daed* would expect anyway. Besides," when she turned to look at him, there was a hint of sparkle that'd once attracted him in the blue. "I figure keeping you and your sandwiches out of the yard will prevent drawing all the county's ants into it." Setting the glass of iced tea before him, she took a seat at the opposite side of the table. With one hand anchoring the cookie to his mouth, Caleb used his other to stabilize himself as he worked his way around the kitchen chairs to where she sat. When he reached her, she pulled him into her lap.

"Do you ever deliver milk to the cheese factory anymore?"

Jonah's last bite stuck in his throat. Picking up the tea, he drained a third of the glass to help wash it down. That was where they'd really gotten to know each other. The cheese factory. She'd had a job there briefly, after her *mamm* had died. He'd been the one from his family's dairy to deliver their milk. One early spring day, he dropped it off when she was on break and, in order to enjoy the sunshine and promise of warmth after a long Wisconsin winter, was eating her sandwich out on the dock. Jonah had known her from school and other community functions, but he hadn't really *known* her beyond the reputation she was already growing. Although attracted—she was, after all, a pretty girl—he hadn't been interested in walking out with her. As he was already a baptized member of the church, the things she was rumored to participate in were things he wouldn't be doing until the other side of marriage.

But when a big diesel truck had pulled into the factory yard, the younger Belgian in his team had spooked. He'd gotten the horses settled quickly, only to find that during the brief ruckus, the empty milk cans had tipped over in his wagon bed, with a few escaping into the yard. By the time he'd secured the team, Lydia had collected the escapees and was waiting to load them back into the wagon. They'd talked as she'd spent the rest of her break helping him reset the milk cans in the bed.

The next day, he'd just *happened* to deliver milk at the same time to find her lunching in the same place. A short time after that, he'd started packing a sandwich and joining her on her break. That'd led to meeting up at other times. His folks had never understood why he'd always insisted on taking the milk in. Or why it took him so long to do so. Or why he'd abruptly stopped.

"*Nee.* One of my younger brothers does now. They're all out of school and working on the farm." He paused. Debated. And mentally shrugged. They used to be able to talk together. They used to do a lot of things together. "One of the things I've been trying to get my *daed* to do is to coordinate with the other Amish dairymen in our and nearby districts, and as a group, hire a truck and driver to pick up the milk at the farms and deliver it to the factory. It would save everyone time from having to make the trip with a team, something of particular benefit during crop season when men and teams are needed in the field. And the factory perhaps, would consider a slight increase on the milk price, as it could be more efficient for them, having fewer and bigger deliveries."

Her eyebrows peaked. "What did your *daed* say?"

"He said he'd think about it."

Her lips curved at his obvious disappointment. "That's not a *no.* Your *daed*'s a reasonable man. He'll see it for the *gut* idea it is when he has a chance to turn it over in his mind."

"I feel like someone his age," he nodded toward Caleb. "Having to deal with a *not now*."

"Well, again, a *not now* isn't a *no*. You seem to think patience is just a name that should be assigned to a girl, like Hope or Charity, and not a virtue as outlined in the *Biewel*." Her smile faded as their eyes locked. Was she thinking the same thing he was? That virtue was something they'd both struggled with. Though her struggle was legion, that didn't negate his own failing.

Brushing crumbs from his fingers, Jonah rose to his feet. "*Denki* for the sandwich. I need to get back to work. Or the virtue of patience is something your *daed* won't feel when I don't get his project done in a timely manner." He headed for the mudroom and turned to pull the door shut behind him. Tipping his head in angle with the closing door, the little boy raised a pudgy hand to wave. Lips twitching, Jonah couldn't resist waving in return. His smile faded as he faced the firmly closed portal. That was the longest conversation he'd had with her since…before.

It'd been *gut*. There'd been glimpses of the Lydia he'd thought he'd known then. The one he'd fallen for. He inhaled deeply. *Be careful*. The Lydia he thought he'd seen might not stay. Or might exist only in his imagination. He couldn't afford to care for her again, not knowing who the woman really was from one moment to the next. One heartbreak was enough.

Over the next few days, Lydia went through the cookbooks in the cupboard to find and make tried-and-true family recipes. To the disgruntlement of her *bruder*, she prepared them for Jonah at lunch, while Jacob and her *daed* had the leftovers for supper. When Jacob complained about it, Lydia, unwilling to change the situation, had responded that at least tasty leftovers should be better than what they'd been eating before she'd returned, when the two men had been left to their own devices. And shouldn't she be hospitable and take care of a community member working in their home? Jacob didn't refute her, just grumbled that he was looking forward to having a wife who was more likely to make him a priority as opposed to a sister who'd do her best not to. Lydia's stomach had clenched at the reminder that she might soon be an interloper in her own home.

Her father just ate the leftovers and smiled. Either he was simply glad not to have to attend to the kitchen tasks himself, or he was thinking that he too would soon have a spouse of his own to do so. Her stomach knotted further.

Lydia was struggling not to feel the coziness of the midday mealtime herself. Although she was trying to be careful, having Jonah at the noon meal, with Caleb contentedly picking away at his own food in the nearby high chair, was too much like a dream she knew she could never allow to come true. A family with Jonah. A dream for her. Perhaps even for him for a while. But one that would eventually turn into a nightmare for Jonah when the inevitable traits she shared with her *mamm* and sister appeared. After all, they'd also, early in a relationship, been able to fool a man into marrying them before revealing their true natures.

She couldn't do that to Jonah. Still, the noon meal quickly became her favorite part of the day, the time she looked forward to as soon as she woke up and the time she reflected upon as soon as the mudroom door clicked behind Jonah when he returned to work following lunch. After he'd cleaned up for the day and before going home to help his family with milking, he'd stick his head in the doorway to say goodbye. They'd chat a bit more. And she'd dream a bit further. Of a time that, instead of hearing his buggy rattle down the lane, she'd hear him come in to wash up for supper.

Foolish, foolish dreams.

Sounds from the new addition no longer made her tense; they made her smile to know he was that close. But just out of reach. He'd always be out of reach for her.

She listened for sounds from that area now. Footsteps that announced his arrival in the mudroom. The rattle of lumber and clink of metal indicating he was setting down tools or whatever supplies he might've finished with. Lydia smiled. She hadn't told him, but every night after he left she went into the area to see what work he'd done for the day. The first day she'd been disappointed he wasn't working faster. Now she was growing dismayed at the progress he was making.

He was an extremely neat worker. Whatever he'd done for the day, he never left a mess behind. Lydia wasn't surprised. That was the way he'd lived life. Disciplined. Principled. Unlike her, who always left a shambles in her wake. Maybe that was the reason she'd been attracted to him? That he was her opposite? Had she been drawn by his confidence in himself due to the lack of it in herself? Or had she been drawn because his adherence to the rules made him a challenge? Compressing her lips, Lydia twisted her hands in her apron. No, she didn't want to think she'd been attracted to a conquest. She wanted to think that what they'd had, for a short, treasured time, had been honest. Sincere. Unselfish. Something rare indeed, for her.

Foolishly, her nervous system didn't seem to realize that whatever they'd had, it was in the past, as her stomach fluttered when the door to the mudroom opened and Jonah stepped in. He gave her a slow smile that caused the fluttering to riot further, before turning his gaze to Caleb in his high chair and on to the two place settings at the table.

"Your *daed* still helping at the neighbor's?"

The fluttering dimmed at the reminder. This would be their last such meal alone together. The last one to dream about. The fluttering faded away completely. Maybe that was a good thing. She swallowed. No maybe about it. It was a good thing. She shouldn't weave dreams about this man. "*Ja*. He figures they'll be finishing up the last field today and he'll be home tomorrow."

"Oh." Nodding in acknowledgment, Jonah went to the sink to wash his hands.

Was he as disappointed as she was? It certainly sounded so. Lydia opened the oven door to check on the casserole, absently noting it still had a ways to go. Now not only was she dreaming dreams, she was hearing what she wanted to hear.

Before he took a seat at the table, Jonah took off his hat and set it on one of the pegs lining the wall near the door. His head was crowned with a circular indentation where his hat had sat, above and below it were unruly curls. Pressing her lips together to forestall a smile, Lydia looked away.

"What is it?"

She shook her head quickly. "Nothing."

Jonah ran fingers through his mashed curls, fluffing them up even further. "You're laughing at my hair."

A snort escaped. "You do have an abundance of it."

"That's better than the alternative." His hands remained in his hair, grasping the ends and pulling the strands to a length that Lydia's eyes widened. Seeing her expression, he sighed. "*Ach*, I do suppose it might be time for a haircut." When she lifted a brow, he acknowledged, "Past time for one."

"I just feel a bit odd sitting in the kitchen with my mother clipping about my ears with the scissors." He grimaced. "Makes me feel like I'm six again."

"Why not have your sisters cut it then?"

Wrinkling his nose, Jonah shook his head, the curls flopping with the movement. "They've got enough on their plates. They don't need my curls as well."

"Well, I don't want your curls on my plate either. But perhaps I'd suffer them on my front porch. I suppose I could cut it for you." As soon as the offer escaped, her mouth remained open as if to call it back.

Her heart pounded under his steady regard. Was he going to say yes? What would she do if he did?

A slow grin creased Jonah's cheek. "That'd be *gut*. Maybe my hat will fit again." He looked around the kitchen. "Now?"

Chapter Six

Now? To camouflage her flaming face, Lydia reopened the oven door and stared sightlessly at the meat-and-vegetable casserole that bubbled in its dish on the rack. Hopefully Jonah would think it was the heat from the oven that flushed her cheeks. Not the prospect of combing her fingers through his curls.

"Is there not time before we eat?" She could hear the creak of the chair under his muscular figure as he shifted.

Did she really want to risk getting that close to him? Or was the fact that she did why the offer had popped out in the first place? How could she possibly sit through the meal now, knowing what would come upon its conclusion? Her stomach wasn't simply fluttering, it tumbled and whirled. With a quick hand, she grabbed her *kapp* ribbons from where they dangled into the oven. *Get a hold over yourself, Lydia. If you don't watch it, it won't just be embarrassment or...excitement that has you burning up.* Deciding the casserole could handle the delay better than she could, Lydia straightened and shut the oven door.

"I think it can stand to wait a bit." After reducing the oven temperature, she retrieved Caleb from his high chair. A quick forage in the cupboard produced some cereal that she poured into a bowl. Shoving his hand through the spill-proof lid with a happy gurgle, Caleb was much more content with the impromptu plan than she was.

She cleared her throat. "If you'll bring a chair out to the porch, we'll get started." Instructing Jonah to place it on the opposite side of the porch from the swing, she set Caleb, along with his blocks, in the space between the kitchen chair and the porch railing where she could keep a close eye on him. Returning to the house, she then gathered—along with her ragged composure—her scissors, a comb, a towel to put over Jonah's shoulders to keep the trimmed hair off his shirt and a broom and dustpan for sweeping up.

Jonah eyed her as he settled in the chair. "Maybe I should've asked first if you know what you're doing?"

Careful not to stab herself with the scissors, Lydia pressed a hand against her stomach. "Maybe you should have," she agreed a bit breathlessly as she stared down at the mop of curls. *Jonah's* curls. As nervous as she was, he'd probably end up with one side of his head shorn close to his scalp while the length on the other side brushed his jawline.

Jonah's glance migrated from teasing to wary. His hand, lean and calloused from his labors, appeared on the crown of his head in momentary protection before he slowly pulled it away, causing further disarray to his locks.

Lydia blew out an extended breath to settle herself. She could do this. It was a head of hair, nothing more. "You should be safe. I've cut my *daed*'s hair since my *mamm* passed away. And my brothers' before that. Their feelings were similar to yours, although their hair was…not." Dubiously, she studied the lengthy ringlets from her position above and behind him. The men in her family didn't have any curls at all. Their hair was straight as the straw in the barn, making it much easier to complete the traditional bowl-cut style of Amish men's hair.

Carefully sliding the scissors into her waistband—she didn't want to set them down with Caleb in the vicinity—she pulled the towel from where she'd tossed it over her shoulder and unfolded it. Biting her lip, she gazed down to where his broad shoulders, only a whisper away, strained the seams of his shirt. With a hard swallow, she gingerly draped the towel over them. It took her another swallow before she leaned closer to adjust the towel in place around the opening of his collarless shirt. A lean that brought her cheek in contact with some of his wayward curls. A lean that filled her nostrils with the scent of soap, sawdust, a faint whiff of cows and something that was essentially Jonah. A lean that made her want to linger. To wrap her arms completely about his neck and rest her cheek fully against him.

It took her a moment to realize how still Jonah was. He was motionless except for the rapid heartbeat under her idling fingers. Snatching her hands back, Lydia jerked upright. At least she was behind him so he couldn't see the heat that climbed into her cheeks. Between it and her red hair, she'd resemble one of the late season tomatoes in the garden.

Following a few steadying breaths, she reached out trembling fingers and tentatively touched one of the dark curls. Her heart rate accelerated at its silky texture. Pulling it to its length, she let go to watch it spring back against his scalp. With one hand, she gently worked the comb over his head while she located the nape of his hairline with the other. Tucking the comb in her waistband, she retrieved the scissors. She extended a lock to what was hopefully an appropriate length and, with a final deep breath, she snipped.

At the feel of her cool fingers at his nape and in his hair, it took Jonah three attempts to swallow before he succeeded. He'd certainly never felt this way when his *mamm* had performed what to him had been an annoying chore. Now, far from it being annoying, he wondered if he could persuade Lydia to give him weekly haircuts. If so, he'd happily sport hair even shorter than the Englisch generally wore, keeping only enough to prevent his hat from sliding off. *If* Lydia was doing the cutting. This was the closest he'd been to her since...well, since.

Maybe it was a *gut* thing that a haircut wasn't a frequent activity. He was having a difficult time this past week remembering to keep his distance. Since Tuesday, their interactions in the kitchen had felt too intimate, too much—when Caleb would crawl over and pull up at his knee—like the relationship he'd dreamed of having with her. It was a struggle to remember this woman had ripped his heart—and his ego—into pieces and dropped them onto the nearest refuse pile.

While others had reacted to her flirty glances and brazen behavior, he'd responded to her expressions when no one was looking. The lost, anxious look in her eyes when she was at the edge of a crowd. The shaky breaths she'd take before a come hither smile would appear on her lips and she'd saunter over to some other man. He'd been taken in by the fallacy those presented. By the ruse that the real Lydia was reflected then and not in her more obvious behaviors.

He scowled. He'd treated her like he might've a creature that'd lost trust in man and confidence in itself. Slow, steady, quiet. He'd started attending singings again—something he hadn't done since he'd been baptized—because she would be in attendance. It quickly became painful to do so. She was different there than when she was away from crowds. Away from other men. *Ja*, it'd troubled him that many of the rumors in the district seemed to come with the tag of "Lydia said," or "I heard from Lydia that" but he'd thought surely that'd been an exaggeration.

He hadn't attended the singings for long.

Not witnessing her behavior there helped keep his illusion. They'd arranged to meet at other times, other places. And then, one day when they'd been fishing at a local pond, he'd kissed her. She'd kissed him back. When it'd gone beyond that, he hadn't thought he was one of many. He'd thought he was special. That what they had together was special. That she felt the same way. He'd almost told her he'd loved her. Had almost asked her to marry him. Had believed that everyone had misunderstood her.

How she would've laughed.

He was the one who'd misunderstood.

But it was hard to recall that when she was running her fingers through his hair. When his interactions with her these past few days reminded him of the sweet ones when he'd been certain everyone else's impressions of her were wrong...

To his relief, Caleb crawled over his boots and started across the painted floor of the porch, distracting him from his disturbing memories. Jolting from his chair, Jonah snagged him before the little boy reached the steps.

"You almost got your ear cut off," Lydia advised as he settled back into the chair. "He'll get hair on him if he's on your lap."

Jonah studied the boy's wispy dark hair. "Looks like he could use some."

"Maybe you didn't have much as a baby either." The comment was accompanied by an abrupt silence behind him. He winced, wondering if he now had a missing chunk of hair in the back of his head. *Ach*, a reason to keep his hat on until it grew back.

"If he sits out here on my knees, he's not going to get much hair on him. Unless you go flinging it about." He frowned at the growing pile of curls on the towel that draped him and the even deeper one on the floor. "You leaving any up there?"

"I think there's a strand or two remaining." After carefully removing the towel from about his neck, Lydia trotted down the steps and shook it into the yard. She cocked her head as she returned to the porch. "Too bad it isn't spring. I think you could've furnished all the nests in the area with what's come off."

Jonah gingerly patted his head. "I'm more worried that you remembered to leave some on."

After swiftly sweeping up the porch floor and storing her equipment, Lydia lifted Caleb to her hip. "There's a small mirror in the bathroom that *Daed* uses for shaving if you want to see for yourself."

Doing as she mentioned, he fingered the shorter locks in his reflection. Bowl cut. Curls somewhat subdued. It looked *gut*. It felt *gut*. And what felt much too *gut* was the fact that she'd done it for him. Jonah sighed into the small mirror. He wasn't concerned about what was lost of his hair. His concern was for the little pieces of his heart that she was again chipping away.

It was like playing I Spy among the weeds for what tomatoes had survived a summer of neglect. It wasn't her *daed*'s and *bruder*'s fault. With the farm, Jacob's job and—Lydia's mouth twisted—their respective courting, it was a wonder the garden had been tended at all. In fact, she was surprised they'd even planted one, as she and Hadassah hadn't been around to do it this spring. But habits and necessity died hard. And she could see evidence where, though weeds had overgrown a good part of the garden, a few potatoes had been dug, some peas had been harvested and several of the cabbage plants were missing their heads. So though the tending may have suffered, produce had still made its way to the table.

She'd been working on the garden when she could these past few days. As she toiled to shape it up, she'd found she was enjoying the process, unlike when she'd been younger under her mother's harsh supervision. Lydia had enjoyed any other chore that'd taken her outside, but the garden had still been her mother's domain. The best times had been when she'd helped with planting or harvest, working outside with her father and older brothers, driving a team of horses so the men were free to do other tasks. She'd felt appreciated. She'd felt valued. Other times she'd trailed after them outside, hoping to be assigned some chore or included in their work, only to be instructed to return to the house where her mother needed her. She hadn't understood why. She hadn't seemed to be able to do anything to suit her mother.

Sitting back on her heels, Lydia compared the garden's current condition versus what she'd have it back to by next spring. At least she'd learned to keep an immaculate garden from her *mamm*. If there'd been one blade of grass encroaching upon the patch then, the girls would've heard about it in no uncertain terms.

Rising to her feet, she turned at a sound coming from the house where she'd left the window open to the room where Caleb was napping. At the sight of Jonah crossing the yard, an instantaneous smile rose before she quickly bridled it.

"Is everything all right?"

"*Ja.* I just ran into a spot where I could use an extra hand." He eyed the tomatoes she held. "If you could spare one for a moment."

"Certainly. But I don't know much about carpentry." Careful to keep a few feet between them, she fell in step beside him as they returned to the house. She didn't want their hands to accidentally brush. Cutting his hair yesterday had been difficult enough. Though she'd eventually attained her equilibrium, it'd taken all her focus and some pretense not to reveal how his nearness affected her. But she was very good at pretense.

"Can you hold a string?"

"Well, *ja.* I think I can manage that."

"That's all that's necessary. I need to check some things for plumb. While my arms are long, they can't quite span the eight feet between ceiling and floor."

One of the mentioned arms swung easily beside her as they walked. It was half of the strong set that'd once held her so tenderly. Why did she have to remember that? Lydia's grip tightened on the tomatoes until she was afraid she'd bruised them. "All right. Let me put these in the kitchen and check on Caleb."

Unlike the original home it was connected to, the *daadi haus* was only one story. Apparently her *daed* had spoken about the addition with the widow he was courting, because at lunch today, he'd discussed with Jonah a move of an interior wall. Jonah hadn't commented on the work he'd already completed that might need undone. He'd just nodded and followed her *daed* out to the addition to review the wall's new location while she'd cleared the table. She smiled ruefully as she ran dishwater into the sink. Would a man ever move a wall for her?

When she checked, Caleb—his little face relaxed in sleep—looked like he'd be napping for a bit yet. Making her way to the addition, Lydia followed sounds until she found Jonah, who looked up from where he was nailing a board to the floor when she paused in the doorway.

He stood. "Ready?"

She slowly ventured into the skeletal room. "I think so. What do you need me to do?"

Jonah pointed to the two-step ladder situated near the secured length of board. "Climb on the ladder and hold the plumb bob at the ceiling from where I tell you to." He handed her a thin coil of string attached to a heavy weight on one end that tapered to a point.

"You're making sure everything is level?"

He smiled at her. "*Nee. Level* is a horizontal term. *Plumb* is a term used for making sure things are straight vertically." He ran his hand up and down like a chopping motion. "You're going to hold the string where I direct you. The weight is going to determine where the top board for the walls needs to be placed in order to be precisely over the bottom board that I've already put down based on your *daed*'s new request."

Climbing to the second step of the ladder, she lifted the string, running it through her fingers at his instruction until the plumb dangled over the edge of the board that was already nailed to the floor. She moved it along the ceiling a few times as he directed, until he called, "That's it. Don't move."

Pulling a flat-sided wooden pencil from his pocket, he stepped onto the first riser of the opposite side of the ladder. A step which brought his face even with hers. The plumb line wavered. "Hold still." His eyes were locked on hers. It was hard to breathe. Why was she suddenly so breathless? Why was he the only one who made her breathless?

Her lips parted. The hand holding the string drifted away from the ceiling.

The plumb bob clattered to the subflooring. Lydia looked up to see her hand dangling in midair. Her face paled. She stumbled from the ladder. The string hung limply from her hand as she hunched her shoulders and lowered her head.

"What's wrong?" The metal ladder creaked as Jonah descended as well. The tips of his work boots appeared at the edge of her downcast vision.

"I'm sorry. I'm so sorry. We'll have to start again. It's all my fault," she whispered to the floor. The back of her nose burned with impending tears.

"Hey." Jonah's voice was as quiet as hers. A gentle finger lifted her quivering chin until her gaze met his concerned one. His chest rose and fell as he drew in a few ragged breaths of his own.

"You're not going to yell at me?" Her voice was as small as she wished she could make herself. A berating, or a bit worse, was what happened when she'd failed on a household chore in the past.

He frowned. "Yell? *Nee.* Why would I yell at you? You should be frustrated with me for not being a little quicker to mark the location and leaving you hanging." He led her back to the ladder. "It's no problem. We'll be even faster this time."

Giving him a brief nod, she sniffed and stepped back onto the ladder.

Jonah forced himself to look away from the tears welling in her eyes. *Please don't cry.* When Rebecca had cried, he'd been uncomfortable, not knowing what to do. With Lydia's blue eyes swimming in unshed tears, there hadn't been any question. He'd had to fist his hands for a moment to keep from pulling her into his arms.

Why had the simple mistake thrown her off so? He knew why he'd had to take steadying breaths. That moment on the ladder, when she'd been so close. When her eyes hadn't held tears, but yearning. A yearning that matched his. Marking the location of the plumb bob had been the last thing on his mind.

He could've marked the ceiling on his own. He had methods to do so, the same ones he'd used for the initial location and all the other walls. But he'd missed the time alone they'd shared before her *daed* joined them for lunch.

He was right; they were faster this time. Lydia found the initial spot almost immediately, carefully keeping her hand still as she leaned away when he mounted the ladder and quickly marked it. He'd moved the ladder to the opposite end of the board already secured to the floor. This time she didn't need direction as she moved the inception location of the string to find the precise edge of the bottom board. As they waited for the weight to become perfectly still, she spoke for the first time since her discomposure at losing their place.

"Do you believe people can change?"

Furrowing his brow, Jonah gave the question the serious consideration her solemn voice indicated it required. "I think it's possible. I think there has to be great motivation and determination to do so. Not everyone who wishes to change has that. But with *Gott*, anything is possible. Look at Saul's conversion to Paul. He went from persecuting Christians to authoring several books of the *Biewel*."

He looked up into her troubled eyes. Drawing in a shaky breath at his response, her lips edged into a tremulous smile.

Jonah felt like he'd been given a prize. They worked silently from then on. Upon making the last mark, he took the string from her—without touching hands—and wound it around the plumb. "You might have a future as a carpentry apprentice."

She soaked up the compliment like an empty puddle in a spring rain. "It feels *gut* to see some kind of definite progress made on each task done. Is that why you like it?"

"That. And I like to create." He shrugged. "To make things better than they were when I started."

"Why don't you add someone to help? You could get even more done."

"I will. Someday. If I stay focused on construction. Though it takes a little more time, most of the tasks I can do by myself." He stored the plumb bob in a large toolbox set against the wall. "Right now, I'm not sure which direction I'm going to go and I don't want to take someone on, then have them need to find another job if I decide to stay in farming." He lifted his hands in an open-palmed gesture. "I like farming too. Like it enough I'm trying to save money to buy a place."

"I know whatever decision you make, it'll be a *gut* one." Her lips slanted. Jonah didn't know whether to interpret it as a smile or a frown. "As I recall, you despised the thought of making a wrong one." She straightened as a cry carried through the open window. "I have to go. Caleb's awake. Thanks for letting me help."

"Thank you for helping." Jonah's words were to the empty room. The thud of the closing mudroom door to the kitchen echoed through the hollow space. He waited for a moment, recognizing when she'd reached Caleb's room when the boy's cries ceased. Listening very closely, he heard the murmur of her voice as she greeted the child.

Drawing in a deep breath, he turned toward the lumber from the disassembled initial wall that he'd stacked earlier along the exterior of the room. Hooking a hand on the short ladder, he pulled it to where he needed to start, recalling as it bumped along how distraught she'd been over a little mistake, and her later question on whether people could change. A piece of the puzzle that was Lydia? His response had been sincere. He felt it was possible, if someone wanted it enough.

Had she changed, from the Lydia who'd left a year earlier? It certainly seemed so. Or maybe she was revealing what her true nature was. The nature he'd thought he'd seen all along, not the one the community knew. Which one was real?

As for him changing? Apparently not. Because if he had, he wouldn't be falling in love with her all over again.

Chapter Seven

"I told you I'd beat you here."

"Only because you were recklessly passing everyone we came upon." Climbing down from his buggy, Jonah refuted his eighteen-year-old brother's claim.

"Ha, look who's talking. Where do you think I learned it from?" Josiah countered. "But it doesn't look like Paul has acquired quite our skill yet." The two older *breider* watched as their younger *bruder* pulled his rig next to where they'd just parked along the growing rows of buggies in the large field reserved for that purpose.

"Give him a break. Your first horse when you were sixteen wasn't that fast either."

"*Ja.* But it didn't take me too long to get a faster one."

"Are you thinking of buying today?" Jonah

had come to look, more for the social atmosphere rather than planning to purchase anything. He liked to ponder an acquisition rather than get caught up buying something in the excitement of an auction. Although, if he found tools or equipment that would be useful for his carpentry business, he might bid if he could get them for a good price.

Josiah's grin widened. "Not when I already have a horse that can beat yours." When Paul and their younger *bruder* Harley jumped down from both sides of the nearby buggy, he tsked. "What took you so long?"

"*Ach,* we had to stop and help all those folks who you'd scared off the road."

Laughing at the comeback, Josiah tipped the brim of Paul's hat down over his eyes. Jerking his hat back up, Paul playfully punched his older brother in the shoulder.

"Boys. Please remember that we are no longer on the farm today. That you are now in public and need to act accordingly." Willa Lapp shook her head at her sons as her husband handed her down from the buggy that'd pulled alongside.

"This is accordingly, *Mamm,*" Paul objected. "If we were in the barn, I'd have hit him a little harder."

His *mamm* sighed. "Too bad behavior isn't

one of the things available for auction today. Although for what it would cost to find a fitting amount to supply you boys, I don't know that we could afford it. Zebulun, I wouldn't have minded if you'd have given me six girls instead of just Hannah and Gail and these four." She nodded toward her sons.

"I'm not sure that any more girls we'd had would've acted much differently," Zebulun deadpanned as he attended to his horse. When his wife tipped down the brim of his hat an instant later, a subtle smile was visible beneath the edge of it.

Jonah echoed his *daed*'s smile. Although his father's unwillingness to implement his ideas frustrated him, he wouldn't trade his family for anything. "I don't suppose we all needed to drive today."

Josiah clapped him on the shoulder. "Even when I do like you, big brother, I don't want to be glued to your hip. There might be a thing or two, or a girl or two, that I'll find interesting today. And I might not want to be pulled away when you decide it's time to go home for your afternoon nap."

Elbowing his brother's unprotected side, Jonah quipped, "You may find them interesting, but it's highly doubtful that they'd find you the same."

* * *

The sounds of bantering faded as Lydia watched the couple and their four sons—ranging in height and build according to their descending ages—through the storm front of her buggy as the group headed down the grassy avenue between the rows of matching black conveyances. She'd just finished changing Caleb and had been repacking the bag she kept in the buggy for that purpose when the series of buggies had arrived and the family had alighted. Her smile at their teasing diminished as they continued toward the growing crowd around the buildings and pens that were housing the expansive auction.

Had her older brothers teased each other as they'd worked together while growing up? Perhaps the three of them had while they'd spent their time employed outside. There'd certainly been no joking at the mealtimes under their mother's stern gaze, which were about the only times the boys had stayed in the house.

On the occasions they'd had company, her *mamm* would put on a different persona. The girls would breathe a temporary sigh of relief, but though nothing was said when visitors were in the home, any perceived offense was still game for criticism to rain down later.

Her *mamm* hadn't been nearly as hard on her sons as she'd been on her daughters. Had that just been Lydia's perception? Or had it been because she'd figured the boys were more under their father's domain? Had she just preferred her sons, believing girls weren't as valuable? Lydia knew other Amish homes didn't feel that way at all. Other homes treasured all their children equally. Why her mother had seemed to act differently, she didn't know. But it was something she wouldn't repeat.

She scooted Caleb, who'd been bouncing on her knees, closer to her chest and encircled his warm, sturdy figure with her arms. "That would make no difference to me. I will always love you dearly regardless of anything. And I will always make sure you never doubt you're loved.

"Jonah has a family like that, doesn't he? You can tell by the way they act together that everyone feels...valued. Loved. Secure in themselves. I wonder what it would feel like to be in a family like that?" She sniffed against the unexpected pricking in the backs of her eyes. "You deserve that. He deserves that, which is why he doesn't deserve me." She sighed. "Pretty dreary thoughts for what's supposed to be a fun outing, huh."

She'd come today with her dad at his encouragement. She scowled. When she'd demurred that she'd rather stay home, the encouragement had edged into a directive. Excited to attend himself, Henry couldn't understand why anyone else wouldn't be. The old Lydia would've agreed. It would've been what was expected of her. It would've been an opportunity to get out of the house for a day. A day of some type of positive reinforcement, regardless of whether that reinforcement was healthy or not. She'd never bought anything at an auction. Prior to her work at the cheese factory, she'd never had money of her own, and then, what she'd earned had been too precious to spend in rapid bidding. Now that she was uninterested in socializing, to her, attending an auction just meant a crowded and noisy day.

Lydia slid open the door with a decided lack of enthusiasm. "As long as we're here, we might as well go see if we can find some… fun then." With Caleb in her arms, she exited the buggy and headed with measured strides toward the crowd in the distance.

She stopped first at the quilts to be auctioned later. After lingering there, she strolled to where household goods were displayed. Perusing a small stack of hand-cranked blenders, her eyebrows peaked when she spied a price marked on a box. *Not something that will find its way into my kitchen anytime soon, even if it goes for a quarter of that price.* Smiling wryly, she shifted Caleb to her other hip and continued through the milling crowd. Ten yards on, she paused at the sight of her *daed* a few booths ahead across the aisle. Though they'd ridden in together, they'd parted ways at the entrance with an understanding to meet back at the buggy later this afternoon. Raising her hand to wave, Lydia returned it to her side when she saw that he wasn't alone.

Of course, no one seemed really alone at an auction, but it was obvious that he was with the woman, pleasantly round with blond hair slipping to gray, who was standing at his elbow. Her *daed*, wearing a bigger grin than Lydia had ever witnessed at home, was lifting a stovetop popcorn popper for the woman's perusal. She, though smiling, was shaking her head.

Was this the widow her father was courting?

Lydia stepped back until she was blocked from view by a stack of portable gas heaters. To the side of the presumed widow, watching the byplay, were two young women of the same height as the woman but with more slender builds. Their hair, what she could see with their *kapps*, was the same blond hair that might've adorned the widow at a younger age.

Her daughters? Were they married, or still at home? Would they be moving in too? Despite the pleasant fall weather wafting through the open-air building, Lydia panted a moment as if her lungs were starved of air. The old fairy tale came to mind, the one about the sweet, righteous girl and her evil stepmother and stepsisters. Only, unlike that tale, she was far from sweet or righteous. Would her father wait to marry until the *daadi haus* was finished? Even then, would there be room for her and Caleb in the household if his new wife had these children and perhaps more coming with her? What would she be like? The woman had a pleasant countenance. But sometimes what a woman was like around a prospective beau was not what she was like after matrimony. Lydia had vivid examples of that with her mother and Lucetta.

Weaving her way in the opposite direction through aisles crowded with people and goods, she finally emerged outside to squint against the morning sun. "What say you to looking at some livestock? Would you like to see cows and horses, maybe some sheep?"

Caleb clapped his hands together. "I'll take that as a yes. Right now, I'd prefer them to people we might know."

Horses, vital to Amish life, were always a big draw at these events. A good driving horse with a solid pedigree could sell for several thousands of dollars. At an auction, in order to make an informed purchase, a buyer would spend a lot of time examining the horses in the pens where they were held prior to being led out for sale. Many owners would allow prospective buyers to ride or drive the animal themselves before the horse was called into the arena. Lydia paused outside an area where several were doing just that, including a girl she didn't recognize riding astride, her skirt pulled out of the way to reveal a pair of jeans underneath.

Lydia stepped into the huge barn, lined with bleachers surrounding a small arena, to hear the rapid cadence of the auctioneer. He and his bid spotters, for there were too many folks in attendance for the auctioneer to be able to see all the bidders himself, were selling a draft team. Listening to the patter, she watched the burly dappled gray Percherons circle the arena. The rapidly rising bid was for the price of a single horse. Unwary buyers might think they were buying both at that price when it was only per animal. When the price was finalized, the auctioneer would inquire whether the purchaser wanted "choice," which meant the buyer would pick which horse he wanted of the pair, or "double the money," which meant he would pay that price for each horse of the team. If the buyer chose choice, then bidding would occur later for the second animal.

In her arms, Caleb began to squirm. "*Ja.* It is a lot of people, isn't it?" Retreating from the crowded barn back into the sunshine, she again watched the horses being tried out prior to purchase. Raising a hand to shade her eyes, she squinted across the makeshift ring.

Beyond a team of chestnut Belgian draft horses that were plodding along the far side, she spied her *bruder* Jacob. With him was a girl she didn't recognize, who must be from another district. The large auction drew several of the surrounding ones. The couple wasn't holding hands, but they were…leaning toward each other. Smiling at each other. Even though her experience had been limited regarding a serious relationship, Lydia could read the signs of mutual attraction. Her stomach hollowed with a contradictory combination of yearning and dread. Yearning for that type of connection herself. Dread with what this might mean for her future. Jacob was serious about this girl. It was evident even across the distance that separated Lydia from her brother. It wouldn't be long before some Sunday morning when Jacob didn't attend their church, but instead went to this girl's home for when the announcement would be made about their upcoming wedding.

Pressing a hand against her stomach, Lydia closed her eyes against the lightheadedness that abruptly threatened. Another woman who would have precedence, soon taking residence in her home. Another one to find fault with her.

Why, with all the folks attending this day, did she keep running into those that she'd rather not? Jacob would've introduced her to the girl, but Lydia didn't feel up to it. Not right now. Not when the quiet house she'd longed to return to was suddenly becoming as crowded with females as the Lapps' dairy barn.

Suddenly fatigued, she skirted along the line of buggies to be sold until she found a quiet place to sit. Setting Caleb down, she steadied him as he used the shaft, the wood worn smooth by years of usage, to lever himself to standing. Inching his way up to where the shaft connected to the buggy and then down to where, currently horseless, its end lay in the grass, he gurgled his enjoyment at being free.

They were out of the way of the crowd. Wrapping her arms about her knees, Lydia watched people pass by. A few were singles like her, though the throng was more likely to consist of groups of twos and threes: men of same age, those of different generations—possibly a father helping a son to pick out his first buggy, women walking with children, some in arms like herself, some with toddlers holding on to their skirts. She saw young women going by, giggling together. That would've been her before she left, chattering with friends she'd connect with at the large outing.

Loneliness percolated through her at the sight. She had closed herself off. In the week she'd been home, she'd borrowed the buggy only once to go to the store for some groceries. The past couple of nights, her *daed* had even suggested she go out. Maybe it was guilt, as he'd been gone a few evenings to visit the widow. He'd even offered to watch Caleb, if Lydia wanted to go to a friend's house.

Lydia didn't. Some of the young women she'd known from before had married in the year she'd been gone. Others, well, had she even really had friends? There were those who'd gravitated to her, avidly listening when she'd spoken of others. But were they really friends? Jealous, envious, gossiping, disregarding other girls' romantic interests when she'd shamelessly flirted; she hadn't been much of a friend herself.

Did you need to be a friend to have one? If that was the case, it wasn't surprising that no one had sought her out since her return. She wouldn't have either. Picking up a pebble from the ground beside her, she tossed it at the wagon wheel where it pinged off the metal banding.

She didn't like the person she'd been. Her mouth quivered. Was that the person she still was? Was the fear of that the reason she'd closed herself off, figuring no one else would like her either? Afraid, that for all the awareness of trying to change in Pennsylvania, she'd fall back into her old habits and actions now that she was back in her home area? *Please,* Gott, *don't let me backslide. Not that I've come that far, but that I've come any distance at all is only through Your grace. I can't do it without Your help.* A tear dripped from her lashes to splatter on her cheek. She dashed it away.

Caleb chortled, breaking her melancholy. Patting the shaft beside him, he grinned at her.

Lydia caught her breath at the sight of him standing by himself with only occasional contact of the shaft. His eyes widened at the slight gasp and her startled expression. He dropped to his bottom on the ground. She scooted to him.

"No, you didn't do anything wrong. I was just surprised. And amazed. Amazed at how much progress you're making." When she offered her index fingers, he gripped one in each little hand and pulled to his feet. "I guess you're showing me that even little bit by little bit, we can move forward. I just hope I can do so with the capability that you do." Though she continued to smile at him, she sighed. "If you're ready to go, we spent the morning dodging folks we know. I suppose, since this is a social event, that we should at least make an effort to be a little sociable."

They rejoined the throng. With eight auctioneers going at the event, there was always something to see. Lydia found her way back inside the building containing household goods, although she kept a wary eye out for her father. Several young women—ones she recognized by face and from the *kapp* style as being from her district—had collected amongst a display of treadle sewing machines. Taking a deep breath, she wandered closer. They all turned to eye her and Caleb. A few just looked and returned their attention to the young woman speaking. Some nodded in greeting and smiled at Caleb. Remembering her realization of needing to be a friend in order to have one, Lydia offered a tentative nod and smile in return.

She didn't need a machine, as her *mamm*'s was still at the house, but she perused them as she tentatively worked her way closer. To her relief, a few of the girls shifted, allowing her to become a part of the group and not left on the outside looking in. She listened to the general conversation regarding who hoped to get a machine of their own and what clothes they were sewing or planning to sew, which led to who might be making a wedding dress. When the conversation progressed to who might be walking out with whom and Jonah's and Rebecca's names were mentioned in tandem, her smile stiffened and she swallowed.

The conversation hushed and the cluster of young women grew tighter as talk turned to who might need to get married soon before a preemptive growing family became evident and whether the schoolteacher, a girl who'd moved into the district a year ago, was as virtuous as she seemed to present when it was rumored she was attending *Englisch* parties.

As she found herself shifting Caleb to her other hip in order to lean in closer to hear better, Lydia was stabbed with the knowledge that a year ago, she'd have been one of those in the center of the crowd, broadcasting whatever tidbit of knowledge she'd collected without thought of those who were the subject. Her heart pounded. Taking a step back, she excused herself to those she'd bumped into in doing so. For a moment, she stood rooted where she could still hear the avid whispers, battling the urge to listen in order to share someone's misfortune with others later. Caleb whimpered in the slight crush.

Lydia looked into his innocent eyes before kissing him on his forehead. "*Denki.* I needed to leave. It was too tempting." Sighing, she politely worked her way completely out of the group.

When she'd moved out of hearing distance, she murmured to him, "I don't want you to think that all are like that. By far and away, many, even most abide by the Proverbs that states 'a talebearer revealeth secrets: but he that is of a faithful spirit concealeth the matter.' I… I was a secret revealer." Turning her back on the group, she pinched the bridge of her nose against the burning at the back of her eyes at the reminder.

When the threat of tears subsided, she lowered her hand to gently tickle Caleb's stomach, drawing comfort from his ensuing smile. "I think maybe I did it because I figured if I was driving the conversation about someone else, at least that way folks wouldn't be talking about me. Not very smart or very nice, huh." She looked past Caleb to where, while several had drifted away as she had, some of the young women still gathered in a small cluster. "It's something I'm afraid I'll have to keep working on."

A final belly tickle was rewarded with a chuckle. "So, what do you say to seeing some physical manure spreaders and leave these verbal ones behind? And who do you think we'll run into there?"

Who they found was not who she expected. As she and Caleb strolled along the rows of farm equipment, they came upon Peter, Lucetta's husband. He was carrying Fannie, whose droopy eyes were red as though tears had been shed in the recent past. Though Malinda initially hid behind her father's legs, she peeked around him when Lydia squatted to her level and said hello. It didn't take much more persuasion for her to come out. Lydia was even able to coax a smile from her. Tired Fannie was a harder sell but eventually responded with one before she rested her head on her *daed*'s shoulder. Lydia looked around, seeking her sister in the nearby crowd.

"Where's Lucetta?"

Chapter Eight

Grimacing, Peter shrugged and shook his head. "I haven't seen her since she handed me Fannie and disappeared. That was an hour or so ago."

Lydia winced. "Will she be joining you again later?"

"I don't know that either. I suppose if she wants a ride home, she'll get back with me. But she's proven she doesn't need me for that either."

Lydia's heart ached for her brother-in-law. He was a quiet, hardworking man who didn't deserve her sister's actions. It was obvious, though he was overwhelmed, that the girls felt secure with him.

"It's past Caleb's lunch and nap time. I have a blanket and some snacks in the buggy. What do you think about laying the blanket on the shady side of the buggy and having a picnic?" *And a nap*, she mouthed to Peter. The girls' eyes rounded at the word *picnic* and they shyly nodded. Peter gave a relieved smile and gestured for her to lead the way.

They passed some of the auction's many food stands as they headed for the buggy. Lifting her nose, Lydia inhaled the tantalizing scents of pork burgers and grilled hot dogs. Though not probable, she imagined she could also smell shoofly and whoopie pies, ubiquitous at these events. Her eyes drifted closed. She hadn't realized how hungry she was.

Opening them, she met Peter's commiserating gaze. "How about we get them settled with a snack to start and one of us goes back for some chips and sandwiches? My treat."

She smiled. "I think that sounds *wunderbar*."

Once they'd reached Lydia's buggy, the little girls established themselves on the hastily shaken out blanket, sharing bananas and crackers Lydia kept in her bag for Caleb. The original plan of sending Peter for the food was stymied by a tired Fannie, who refused to be parted from him. Instead, Lydia quickly fed and tended to Caleb. In short order, he drifted off to sleep. Peter supplied her with some money while he settled on the blanket with the children and she hustled back down the rows of buggies to the tents from which the mouthwatering scents were generating.

Making her way to the end of one of the many lines, she scanned the surrounding area. At the sight of Jonah and Rebecca, along with a few other *youngies* from their district sitting at one of the nearby picnic tables set up for the event, she froze. Hoping they didn't notice her in return, she turned away, but before she could succeed, Rebecca raised a hand in a casual wave. Summoning a smile, Lydia waved back before pretending the hand-printed menu board absorbed all her attention. Which it didn't, because she could feel the growing crush of the line behind her. It pressed closer and closer as she placed her order and paid the harried attendant at the counter. Glancing over her shoulder, she saw a cluster of young men, ones she identified as being from a district in the next county based on the brim width and style of their hats. One of them was openly staring.

"Aren't you that redheaded girl from Miller's Creek?" His smile should've appeared friendly, but it didn't.

Lydia's heart began pounding. Her grip on the sacks of food she'd just been handed slipped in her dampening palms. She didn't recall ever seeing the man before, but she recognized the look. Though charged with instant energy, she knew she couldn't run. Wouldn't run. To do so would make a scene, something she definitely shied away from with Jonah looking on. Still, all she could think about was getting back to Caleb.

Inhaling a shaky, albeit quiet, breath, she pasted on a smile. "Well, I can hardly deny I'm a redhead when the evidence is pretty obvious. Though we may be few, there's actually more than one of us from Miller's Creek."

The man snorted. "I've heard about you. I heard that you were back. You're the very, *very*, friendly one."

Lydia drew the bags of food to her chest as if they could provide some type of barrier. "It's a friendly community."

His gaze drifted to where her hands clutched the bags, pausing there a moment before returning to her face. "Well, I'm friendly too. I'd like to invite you to return to what I hear were your favorite activities."

A bead of sweat trickled down her back. "I appreciate the offer—maybe some other time." Lifting the bags of food, she took a step away. "I'm already meeting someone and I'm sure he's getting more than a little impatient." She forced coquetry into her expression. "I can't wait to get back to him myself. He was reluctant to let me leave in the first place. Only did because we were both so very… hungry." Though she put a titillating emphasis on the word, Lydia had to swallow against the nausea that churned in her stomach. If she didn't get away soon, she was going to be ill.

No matter where Jonah tried to look, his gaze kept returning to Lydia, standing in line at the concession. He saw the apprehension that grew on her face at the press of the *youngies* behind her. Half rising from the picnic table's wooden bench, he drew the attention of the rest of those at the table, including Rebecca and her seatmate Grace Kauffman, Miller's Creek's schoolteacher. Rebecca raised her eyebrows.

"I…uh… Do you need a refill of your tea?"

Her brows puckered as she considered her full glass. "*Nee.* I'm *gut.*" Jonah understood her confusion as he sank back onto the seat. He was confused himself. Lydia was none of his business. This was the woman he should be attending to. And yet…his gaze flicked back to the men surrounding Lydia. He could see her face between two sets of shoulders. A smile was pinned on her lips, but the look in her blue eyes was far from happy.

Grabbing his own full glass, he chugged

half of it down and sprang once more to his feet. "Well, I'm going to get a refill." Swinging his leg over the picnic table's bench seat, he headed toward the concession stand.

Making his way to a nearby counter for condiments, Jonah poured sugar in his cup, just to have something to do while he determined his next move. As he threw in a slice of lemon, he thought he heard the thread of tension in her voice. Preparing to step into the conversation, he paused, his shoulders stiffening when her tone turned unquestionably flirty. The inflection was like a knife twisting in his gut.

He stared at the mess of sugar and lemon he now had in his cup. Where had she met this man she was so eager to get back to and share a meal with? Jonah could've sworn she'd barely left the house since she'd been back, though he'd only been there during daylight hours. Had she been going out at night with Lucetta after all?

Dropping the cup in the trash, he stepped in line to purchase another drink. As he left the counter, he turned to watch, along with the other men, as Lydia walked away, her hips swaying under her dress.

Tea splashed over his hand as he pivoted to head back to the picnic table. What was he doing? He'd been sucked right back into believing she was something she wasn't. Thinking she was sweet like the sugar when she was actually more sour than the lemon, sour for him anyway. When would he learn? Because of her, he'd already broken the vows he'd made to God and his church when he was baptized. And for what? Just to continue to prove his weakness of the flesh? Well, no more. He was finished being a fool over Lydia Troyer.

Sliding onto the picnic table's wooden bench, he gave Rebecca such a smile that her eyebrows rose.

Lydia proceeded through the eating area and passed four parked buggies before she finally stopped shaking. She was glad she'd requested lids on the drinks she'd almost forgotten on the counter. Otherwise they'd have been half spilled, the way her hands had trembled as soon as she'd escaped from the men.

But as she stepped between the buggies to where Peter sat next to the dozing trio of little ones, she made sure none of that was reflected. Rising at her approach, Peter relieved her of some of her burden.

"Any problems?"

"*Nee.* Everything was fine." She settled

onto the blanket, careful not to disturb the sleeping children. "Here?"

"So far, the best part of my day." But as he sat back down, his tender smile when he looked at his daughters belied the words.

"Maybe I could help make it a little better. I've seen about all I want to see and am ready to sit for a while. How about I stay here with the children while you explore more of the auction?"

"I…couldn't…leave you here while I…"

Lydia smiled at the immediate excitement in his eyes when she'd made the offer. "*Ja.* You can. And I think your sandwich and drink will travel well with you if you want to get a head start."

He still hesitated. "If you're sure…"

"For sure and certain."

Peter scrambled to his feet. "There was a piece of farm equipment I was interested in. I'll be back as soon as possible."

"Take your time," she said to his back as he ducked into the grassy avenue and hurried back the way she'd just come. And she meant it. With a sigh, Lydia wrapped up the untouched sandwich she'd lost her appetite for and set it aside for when the children woke. Extending her arms behind her, she leaned back on them out of the shade of the buggy and closed her eyes to absorb a moment of peace in the fall's gentle sunlight.

A short time later, she blinked them open when she sensed a shadow fall over her face. Recognizing the young man blocking the sun as the one from the concession stand, she lurched upright. Uneasy being seated while he loomed over her, she slowly rose to stand between him and the sleeping children.

"Where's your dinner date?"

"He'll be back shortly."

He eyed her solitary drink and the sandwich bag set next to an obvious child's pack. "Sure he will." He smirked, taking a step closer. "Don't tell me the things I've heard about you weren't true."

Lydia held her ground, though her heart rate ran rampant.

"Oh, Lydia! I'm glad you're here. I was wondering if you'd mind lending me a hand with the twins."

Looking past the man who blocked her, Lydia saw a dark-haired young woman had paused in the makeshift street between the rows of buggies. On either side of her were toddlers, a boy and a girl, who each had one hand fisted in the bottom of her dress and the other one wrapped around one of the woman's fingers.

Lydia's chin sagged. Amongst all the folks she was most ashamed to see, Rachel Raber would top the list. Before she'd left for Pennsylvania, Lydia had been horrible to the woman, spreading rumors and insinuations. When she remained speechless, the woman and little twins ambled closer. As they did, Lydia's interloper stepped back.

"*Ja.* I'd be glad to help." Lydia pitched her voice just loud enough for her call to get past the young man. Grimacing, he ducked into the thoroughfare and, following a last look in her direction, hastened away.

Rachel and her children continued their approach. Reaching the edge of the blanket, one of the twins released his grip on his mother and her skirt to pick a blade of grass with tiny fingers. The other dropped to her knees and patted the soft surface of the blanket.

Lydia watched the woman's deft handling of the little ones. "You were fine with the twins by yourself."

"That may be, but I always appreciate a little help." Rachel grinned. "For sure and certain, they took some getting used to."

Glancing at sleeping Caleb, Lydia nodded and smiled in understanding. "One at a time is a challenge enough. I can't imagine two."

They lapsed into silence. Hanging her

head, Lydia shifted her feet under the woman's quiet regard.

"Rebecca told me how kind you were to her when she was worried about our *mamm*."

Lydia jerked her head up. "I'm glad, so very glad, to hear that your *mamm* and the *boppeli* are doing all right."

Rachel's sweet smile made Lydia understand why her husband, Ben, could have always loved the girl, even when she'd been walking out with his brother. "*Ja*. This little one is going to be all right. Praise *Gott*."

They shared a warm glance.

"I always admired your *mamm*," Lydia blurted. Heat crept into her cheeks but she continued. "I always envied you. You had her for a mother and it seemed any boy that you wanted. More than any. I'm sorry." She bit her lip. "I'm sorry for any pain that I'd caused you."

Now a flush rose on the dark-haired woman's cheeks. "It is all forgiven. I just wanted my one special someone. Ben wasn't the one I expected, but he is *Gott*'s chosen one for me, for which I am truly, truly thankful."

To Lydia's surprise, Rachel reached out to grasp her hand. "I hope you find His one for you as well. Sometimes it takes a route you don't expect."

Lydia shook her head. She figured *Gott* would spare any good man from being tied to her for life. "I don't expect to find one."

"*Gott* has a plan. We just have to discover what His will is for us." Releasing Lydia's hand, Rachel's gaze dropped to the twins, who were making themselves at home on the blanket. She sighed the sigh of a woman chasing toddlers. "I'm finished for the day. Ben will be here shortly if you don't mind me and the twins keeping you company until he arrives."

Lydia's stomach clenched momentarily. She'd flirted with Ben Raber when he'd been a married man. His rightfully shaming her had been one of the things that'd prompted her departure for Pennsylvania. But was Rachel offering friendship? If so, it was something Lydia felt in desperate need of. She gestured toward the blanket. "I'd be glad of your company. And I thank you for the earlier rescue."

"Oh, thanks definitely go to the twins." There was a twinkle in Rachel's eye. "They intimidate everyone when they arrive."

When Ben found them a short time later, Lydia was leaning against a wagon wheel, with all five children huddled on or about her lap as she read a picture book she'd brought along for Caleb. Stiffening at the sight of her, Ben darted a concerned glance toward his wife.

"Everything all right?"

Rachel pushed up from where she lounged on the blanket. "Everything is very *gut*. Very *gut* indeed." Taking the hand her husband offered, she rose to her feet.

"I do hope you'll consider coming to the cider frolic next Saturday, Lydia. And later, to the canning frolic we're having for my *mamm*."

"*Denki.* I'll definitely keep them in mind."

Rachel and Ben each lifted a twin into their arms. "Would you like us to wait with you until Peter or your *daed* returns?"

"Oh, *nee*, Rachel. We'll be fine."

"Well, then, *mach's gut.* We'll see you at church next Sunday, if not before."

"Rachel?"

The young woman looked back with an inquiring smile.

"Thank you again for…for stopping. I didn't expect to find anything at the auction today. But you've given me more than I could've imagined."

Rachel's smile widened. "You are welcome, Lydia. It was my pleasure." At Ben's frown, she patted him on the shoulder. "I'll explain on the way home."

Chapter Nine

Lydia spooned more peas onto Caleb's tray. For every one he managed to stuff into his mouth, he scattered two more amongst the macaroni and banana bits that were already strewn over the white plastic surface. Lifting the serving bowl, she glanced at her *daed*. Jacob was out, with friends or courting his girl, Lydia didn't know. It was just the three of them for supper, as it had been for dinner. To her disappointment, Jonah hadn't sat down for the meal, instead sticking his head in the door to announce he was going into town for supplies. She'd smiled at him, but he'd evaded her gaze.

"More peas?"

Her *daed* shook his head. Though Lydia dropped her attention to her food, she felt the weight of his gaze. She chased her own peas around her plate.

"No one came yesterday while I was… out?"

Lydia suppressed a rueful smile at her *daed*'s question. He seemed embarrassed by his courtship of the widowed woman now that Lydia was home. She hadn't told him she'd seen them together the other day at the auction. Them and the woman's daughters. Her smile quickly faded as she considered the end of the courtship, when he married and brought someone home to live with him. Presumably with her. Isolating some peas, she pressed them under her fork. Any desire to eat had fled.

Where would she go, if she couldn't stay here? Few young men would want to marry into a ready-made family, particularly with a woman of her reputation. How many children might this widow have who would also be moving into the house? Was that why *Daed* was so keen on having the *daadi haus* built before they moved in? And then there was Jacob, who would marry at some point and want to raise his own family in the house. Where would that leave her, and Caleb?

"*Nee*. No one stopped by." Why would they? As she'd already realized, she hadn't really been a friend to anyone. She had nothing to tell those who might be intrigued by gossip, and previous victims of her gossip certainly weren't likely to seek her out. Her lips lifted in one corner. Except Rachel. Saturday with her had been very…nice. Was that what friendship was like?

Henry frowned. "You should be out more, seeing other young folks. Maybe find a job."

The silverware clinked as Lydia set it on her plate and gently nudged both away. Was she not doing the housework sufficiently to suit him? Would he rather be living in a bachelor house, or simply wait for the widow to arrive rather than have Lydia prepare the meals and keep up the house? As a litany of all her mother's criticism scrolled through her mind, the backs of Lydia's eyes burned. Unwilling to have her *daed* witness any tears, she was grateful when Caleb banged his hand on his tray. Turning in his direction, she pointed out to the boy some of the morsels he'd missed.

She cleared her throat. "I'll try to do better here. Is there something that hasn't been done the way you'd prefer? The laundry? My cooking? The house upkeep? The garden?" All had been areas her mother had admonished.

Lydia cringed as Henry's chair scraped on the linoleum when he pushed back from the table. Hunching her shoulders, she waited as he walked around it. Fortunately, Caleb was currently satisfied, as she couldn't do much more than drop her shaking hands into her lap.

She flinched at the weight of her father's hand on her shoulder. Compressing her mouth into a tight line to stop its quivering, she lifted her gaze to the censure on his face.

It wasn't there. What was, was…compassion? At the sight, the tears leaked from the corners of her eyes.

"Oh, *dochter*, what have we done to you?" Her *daed* gave her shoulder a gentle squeeze. He'd never touched her before. She'd seen him pat the shoulders of her *breider* over the years, but he'd never put a hand, comforting or not, on her. Neither had her mother. But Lydia might've preferred that to her whipping words that left unseen, but equally damaging, scars.

"You have been doing a fine job at the house. It's been *gut* to have regularly laundered clothes again, and to enter into a clean house after a day of work and smell the *gut* food you've prepared. But I worry that you're isolating yourself here when it would be helpful for you to get out of the house once in a while. To meet others, to perhaps meet a young man so you could…" He waved his other hand in a small circle, as if Lydia could surely understand what he meant by meeting a young man.

She did. He was trying to get her married off and out of the house. That's what he meant.

"You're taking excellent care of the boy." Her *daed* smiled at Caleb. "But if he is what's keeping you at home, perhaps you could give him into Lucetta's care for a time for you to seek a job, or meet some folks your age. As a married woman already home with young children of her own, it wouldn't be such a major transition to her life."

Bracing a hand against her stomach, Lydia struggled to breathe in a room that was suddenly stifling. The prospect of her sister raising Caleb was unthinkable. She could already see the effect Lucetta was having on her nieces. Their shyness, their hesitation of doing something wrong that might arouse consequences. Lydia was finally able to take in some air. Caleb would not grow up in an environment like the one she had.

Her mouth dry, she shook her head. "Caleb's not going anywhere." She panted a few breaths before she added the next words. "He's mine."

"I understand having taken care of him this long that you'd feel a connection. I'm proud of you for taking in your cousin's child. The loss of her only daughter would've been devastating for Mary."

Lydia swallowed against a bite of nausea at the words.

"And at her age, she might not feel up to caring for the boy. But you've done enough by bringing him back to family. Your sister has girls close to his age—they can grow up together."

Lydia lurched to her feet. "*Nee*. You don't understand. *I* never said Caleb was Clara's—" her throat almost closed up on the name "—boy. That is just what everyone assumed. And I let them. Maybe that was wrong. One of the *many* wrong things I've done. But Caleb is *not* Clara's. He's *my* child. *My* son." Her face heated under her *daed*'s stunned stare. Squeezing her eyes shut, Lydia drew in several breaths before clearing her throat and continuing with something she should've confessed much, much sooner.

"I knew I was with child when I left Miller's Creek. That was one of the reasons I was willing to go. And I didn't plan to ever return." She'd since learned a harsh lesson that things didn't always work out the way you intended.

Henry drew back, his hand slipping off her

shoulder. Lydia felt its loss all the way down to her toes. His face was still slack with surprise, his mouth opening and shutting a few times although no words were spoken. There was no longer any evidence of compassion in it. Lydia's shoulders drooped at the loss.

Staggering to a nearby chair, her *daed* sagged into it. He looked at Caleb as if really seeing the boy for the first time. Lydia stepped closer to the high chair, instantly preparing to protect should he say anything about her son. Her *daed* could say and think what he wanted about her, but not about Caleb, who was innocent of wrongdoing. Braced to react, she watched as Henry extended a forefinger toward the boy. Delighted at the new source of attention, Caleb grabbed it with sticky fingers. The pair regarded each other across the little boy's messy tray. When Caleb released the finger, Henry used it and an additional one to walk across the high chair tray like the fingers were legs until they nudged an abandoned macaroni. Giggling, Caleb picked up the noodle and popped it into his mouth.

"You were baptized before you left." Despite his smile for the boy, Henry's voice was solemn.

Lydia swallowed. *"Ja."*

"Were you baptized before…?" Her *daed* kept his gaze on Caleb.

"*Ja*," she repeated, her voice barely above a whisper.

Her *daed* turned to her, his eyes conveying a disappointment that hollowed Lydia's stomach. "You broke the vows you made at your baptism. Fornication is a sin. You'll need to confess." He sighed. "Unfortunately, given my role and the evidence of your sin, a free will confession to me alone won't be enough. I'll talk to the deacon and the bishop. But," his gaze slid again to Caleb, "you'll probably need to make a kneeling confession in front of the church. You and your young man."

Lydia sank into her chair, unsure whether her knees would hold her at the pronouncement. "He won't. I… I won't tell who it is."

Henry's jaw sagged. "He refuses to accept the boy as his son?"

She was relieved, given her reputation, that her *daed* was certain she knew who the father was. Maybe he turned a blind eye, like he had when she was growing up, to what was going on in his household. He seemed oblivious to what was going on in the community now. Or maybe he just didn't want to know Lucetta was emulating their mother and had a strained relationship with her husband. And speaking of being oblivious…

"He doesn't know."

Henry's teeth clicked together. "What do you mean, he doesn't know? A man needs to know about his children. And take responsibility for them."

"*I'm* taking responsibility for my actions. That's," she inhaled a long breath, "something I learned, too late, to do when I was in Pennsylvania." Seeing her *daed*'s jaw flex, she licked her lips and continued. "It's better for the father that he doesn't know about Caleb. I don't want him locked in a marriage in case…" Her chin quivered. "In case I'm like my mother."

Henry's glare instantly softened. "Oh, child. You're not."

"How do you know?" Lydia's breath shuddered as she grasped on to the possibility.

"I…don't," he conceded, grimacing. "Only that if you're aware of the nature you want to avoid, you're at least beyond your *mamm*'s understanding of herself."

"Why did you marry her?" Lydia had always wondered. She didn't ask why he stayed married. Divorce wasn't an option for an Amish couple.

Henry ran his fingers through his beard.

"The woman I married turned out to be different than the one I thought I was courting. At first, I thought she was just trying to adjust to wedded life. We both were. After a while, I discovered there was no adjusting for her. It was me who needed to adjust. I dealt with it by staying away from the house as much as was possible. She was more...tolerable in small doses. When the boys got older and their presence seemed to agitate her, I took them out with me. I was thinking that it was because they were rowdy and that you girls—being a bit quieter—would have a better time of it." He shook his head. "I was wrong. For that, I'm sorry."

Her *daed* had never apologized to her before. Lydia didn't know how to respond. The kitchen was quiet except for the ticking of the clock on the wall. Caleb broke the silence by swiping his hand across his tray and sending peas, macaroni and banana bits to rain down over anything nearby.

"His dinner manners need a bit of work." Henry bent to brush some of the bits of food from his pants.

Springing from her chair, Lydia hastened to the sink to retrieve two damp cloths, one for her *daed* and then the floor and the other for the baby and tray.

"You have to tell the boy's father."

She handed him a damp cloth. "I can't. I won't."

Henry sighed. "Then there's no way around it. I'll need to contact the bishop to call for a Members' Meeting. A kneeling confession may be the least of what is required." He rubbed a hand over his face. "As you are denying a father the rights and responsibilities of his own son, you'll need to face the appropriate punishment. Including the possibility of a ban."

Lydia ducked her head as she began to clean Caleb up. She could more easily accept being shunned than tie Caleb's father to a lifelong unhappy marriage. As her *daed* had said, he couldn't be certain that she wouldn't be like her mother was. Like her sister continued to be.

Caleb grimaced while she cleaned his face, before rewarding her with a smile when she was finished. Lydia caught her breath at the sight before returning it with one of her own. She hadn't sought the lie regarding who Caleb's mother was. But she hadn't corrected it either. Though it would cause other questions, other gossip, other—she bit her lip—problems, she was glad the truth was out. She loved her son. She…loved his father. Which was why he'd never know that he was.

* * *

The words behind him were a blow to Jonah's stomach. Regardless of the half-empty soda before him on the Formica tabletop, his throat was suddenly dry. He sat, frozen, in the drive-in's molded seat, oblivious to the hubbub around him, except where all his attention was suddenly focused on the conversation in the next booth.

He'd nodded to the seated couple when he'd come in, recognizing them as being from a nearby district. His *mamm* and *daed* having left the boys to their own devices when they went to visit his sister Gail and her family, he and his brothers had come in for burgers after milking.

"*Ja.* The *boppeli* Henry Troyer's daughter brought back from Pennsylvania is actually hers and not her cousin's like it was thought."

Sweat beaded on his forehead at the words. He kept facing forward, staring at the brightly lit menu above the distant counter, although everything in him wanted to swivel his head and demand more information.

"Where'd you hear that?"

"Henry has been seeing a friend of mine's *mamm*. The girl just told her *daed* the other night when he suggested she have her married sister take the boy."

The conversation moved on in indistinguishable murmurs, or maybe it was just the roaring in his ears. His heart lurched at the thought of Lydia being separated from Caleb. She was devoted to the little boy. Now with what had been said behind him, the reason why was obvious.

How had he not seen it?

If Lydia was Caleb's mother… His heart began galloping. His breath came in gusts. Was he the boy's father? It was possible. Jonah's fingers twitched as he calculated the age he'd heard Caleb was and began counting back the months. His hands fisted. It was very possible.

His jaw clenched. It was also possible for a number of other young men in the area to be the child's father as well.

"You going to eat your fries?"

Josiah's question jolted Jonah's attention back to the table. From his *bruder*'s expression, it wasn't the first time he'd asked the question.

"Nee." Jonah shoved the cardboard container across the table.

"You all right?" Paul eyed him with concern. "You look a little pale."

Josiah scrutinized the two fries he'd just dipped into ketchup. "If these made you sick, I don't want them."

"*Nee.* Just…thinking." Jonah swallowed. *Thinking that I might be a father. Thinking that the girl I cared enough about to give myself to just proved herself to be untrustworthy. Again.*

His legs tightened as he almost rose from the booth to drive to Lydia's house and confront her. Settling back into the seat, he placed a hand on his knee to still its bouncing. He'd wait until morning to get the truth. After all, she'd waited all these months before she'd told it. But he knew it was going to be a sleepless night.

Chapter Ten

Lydia didn't need to check the clock to see that Jonah had arrived earlier than usual. The sky to the east was still extending the first rays of light across the dawn. He must've gotten the cows up early indeed for him to arrive at this time. And as soon as she saw Jonah emerge from his buggy this morning, Lydia knew the reason for the schedule change.

He *knew*.

She hissed in a breath. It'd only taken a few days for the news of Caleb's parentage to filter through the community. She shouldn't be surprised. She knew how fast gossip could travel. She'd been one who'd sent it on its speedy way before.

Lydia stepped back, though her knuckles whitened in her continued grip on the edge of the sink as Jonah marched to the house, his set face fixed on the kitchen window. Her heart rate accelerated as the outer door to the mudroom shut—not a bang, but a sharp click. Two seconds later there was an equally decisive rap on the room's door to the kitchen.

Letting go of the sink, Lydia clasped her hands in front of her. Though she realized this confrontation would happen at some point, she wasn't ready for it.

But she knew what she had to do.

At least her father wasn't around this morning. He'd been quiet the past few days since discovering she wasn't just Caleb's caretaker, but his mother. He hadn't pressed her again as to who Caleb's father was—a relief, as it hurt to disappoint him—but he'd cast her troubled looks and she'd seen him studying the boy, like the little one might have the answer.

Regarding looks, the one Jonah blazed at her upon opening the door almost had her grasping the sink edge again to stay upright. After his gaze pinned her, he glanced about the kitchen until he found Caleb in the corner with his blocks. If his initial expression hadn't shaken her, the look he gave her son would have.

It was everything she could've wanted her son to receive from a father. Everything she could never accept from this man.

His focus back on her, Jonah took a step into the kitchen. "When were you going to tell me?"

Bracing herself, Lydia tipped her head, as if puzzled. "That I'm Caleb's mother? I didn't intend to make it a secret."

Though he didn't take another step, Jonah's weight shifted forward. "That *I* may be his father."

"*May be*," Lydia emphasized as she crossed her arms over her chest, hoping the action would camouflage her tremors. "But you're not."

Sucking in a breath, Jonah's gaze narrowed on her. "How do you know?" he challenged.

"A woman knows these things." Although she hadn't. The majority of her mother's communication with her daughters had been diatribes and none of them had included any information regarding such matters. Lydia had since learned many things from the midwife who'd assisted her in Pennsylvania.

"Did you think you were the only one?" The words hurt, her as much as him as Lydia watched a spasm cross Jonah's face before he controlled his expression. Though she wanted to contort her own countenance in empathy, she forced a smirk upon it. Better that Jonah was embittered rather than offer him—or herself—hope. And better to do it quickly. She didn't know how long she could hold up if he continued to challenge her.

"I was with so many other men around the time I was with you, it would've been impossible to tell. *If* that was the time period. Which it wasn't."

No one here knew Caleb's actual birth date, and she would keep it that way. Lydia kept her eyes overly open, striving to keep tears at bay. Again, she fought the urge to wince when Jonah's strong throat bobbed in a hard swallow. Aching to reassure, she tightened her arms about herself to keep from reaching out to him.

At least this lie was for a good reason. This lie would keep Jonah safe from being trapped in a disastrous marriage with her. This lie would give him a chance to build a life with someone else, someone more...worthy of him.

"Are you going to marry him? The father." The words were hoarse.

"Nee." That, at least, was the truth.

Jonah sagged back on his heels. He seemed to sag, period. Rubbing a hand over the lower half of his face, his gaze again found Caleb. "What about him? Doesn't he deserve a father?"

He does, oh, he does. Though her eyes burned, Lydia was afraid to blink. Afraid it would allow tears to leak. "He has me. I'll take care of him."

With a curt nod, Jonah turned to disappear through the open doorway.

"Who's going to take care of you?"

Had she heard the words, or simply imagined and wished them before terse footsteps crossed the mudroom's concrete floor and the new door to the addition closed with a controlled finality? On shaky legs, Lydia crossed the floor to quietly shut the kitchen door. As soon as it was closed, she braced her back against it and slid to the floor.

Caleb, obviously troubled by the tension in the room, relaxed at this new game. He scampered on his hands and knees over the linoleum to join her. Lydia pulled him onto her lap.

"I thought it was for the best. I cared too much for him and couldn't afford to let him care for me. I went to be with someone else, making sure he'd see me. I almost went through with being with the other man because I despised myself so."

She traced a finger down Caleb's petal soft cheek. "You do deserve a father. Without an obligation to me, he'll choose wisely for a wife. Maybe you would be better off with him and whomever he might choose as a special someone." The tears finally escaped. "But I can't bear to let you go. It was hard enough letting him."

Keeping a palm lightly gripped on the handle of his fishing pole, Jonah propped his elbows on the grassy bank of the pond, closed his eyes and filtered out the dialogue of his fellow fishermen discussing that afternoon's cider frolic. Thankfully the warm weather was lingering into later September and the ground under his elbows, while cool, wasn't uncomfortably chilly. Not like his thoughts.

His gut still ached from when Lydia had told him he wasn't Caleb's father. His hand flexed on the cork handle. An odd twinge of disappointment still hummed through him when he should've simply been flooded with relief and rejoicing at his narrow escape.

Then there was the hollow feeling that she'd taken such pains to ensure he didn't harbor any misconception, like she detested the very possibility of him as Caleb's father. To call the current atmosphere in the Troyer house strained would be an understatement. The past few days, he'd brought a sandwich from home for lunch again, explaining to

Henry that his remaining in the addition to eat it and get immediately back to work was because he was behind schedule. Henry had frowned, but hadn't commented. He'd seemed as in a hurry to get the project finished as Jonah now was. As for what Lydia thought about his not coming in for dinner, he didn't know and he didn't care.

Jonah brushed away a fly that was buzzing by his ear. He did care. That was the problem. How was Lydia going to manage as an unwed mother? He'd been a young teenager when his sister Gail had left home to join the *Englisch*, also, they'd learned later, as an unwed mother. Although he hadn't asked her directly, he'd heard her conversation with his sister, Hannah, about how hard the time had been, carrying all the worries of raising a child on her own.

Even so, she'd done a wonderful job with his niece Lily. He could tell Lydia was doing the same with Caleb. Gail had since returned to the Amish and married the local horse trader, Samuel Schrock, so she now had help, along with another child. But who was going to help Lydia? Not that she didn't have her family around. But it wasn't the same as having the babe's father. Would Caleb's father step up and do what was right for his son?

Would Henry even let Lydia and Caleb stay in his house? Their presence could make his role—a lifelong one—as minister a little difficult. He'd seen what Gail's unexpected departure did to his folks. Whether justified or not, a child's actions were reflected on the parents. While most folks were kind, not everyone had been. After that experience, he'd always tried to ensure that he didn't do anything to cause his parents distress regarding his behavior. His lips quirked. Except perhaps not agreeing with his dad about farm business.

Jonah drew in a deep breath, any inclination to smile dying away. And except for his time with Lydia. A time when he'd broken his vows to *Gott* and his church family and could've become the father to her child. But obviously hadn't.

Opening his eyes, Jonah stared across the quiet water of the large kidney-shaped pond. His gaze ranged up a hill on the far side to the shade of some ancient oak trees. This had been a common rendezvous spot for him and Lydia, whenever they could get away together. Had it been for her and others as well? Just how often had Lydia come here to go "fishing"?

He glanced at the young men sprawled

along the pond's bank, their poles held in relaxed hands. Had she been here with one, or several of them? His stomach churned at the thought. He'd known almost all of them his entire life. They were good friends, most were hard workers, but would they be a good father for Caleb? Or husband for Lydia? Would they understand her, care for her? It was concerning, as easily as they'd taken advantage of her, though some would say she'd taken advantage of them. Had she already told, whomever it was, that he was a father like she'd adamantly told him that he wasn't?

"Enough gabbing about the cider frolic tonight. Did you all hear that Lydia is the mother of that little boy? Not her cousin like it's been said?"

Jonah jerked his fishing rod involuntarily as he zeroed in on the speaker to see if the young man was looking his way, but the *youngie* was staring at his own red-and-white bobber that floated on the pond's still surface.

Another youth leaned forward to rest his elbows on his knees. "My sister figured the boy is at least eight months old. Lydia's been gone not much over a year. That means the boy's *daed* is from Wisconsin."

Jonah's teeth ground together. He wanted to insert that *the boy's* name was Caleb. He kept his mouth shut. Obviously, he hadn't been the only one counting out the months.

Someone tossed a pebble into the pond.

"You're scaring the fish."

"*Ach*. It's not the fish that should be scared. It's the one who might be the father of the boy and stuck with Lydia as a wife."

Jonah silently listened to the banter as he watched the circular ripples expand over the water. Lydia as a wife wouldn't be such a tragedy.

"I'm so glad I didn't do anything more than just kiss her."

There was a chorus of response to the comment. "You said—!"

"*Ja*, I know what I said. But I didn't. Everyone else was saying they had. I didn't want to be the only one she'd turned down when it got to that point."

Jonah's head whipped in the young man's direction.

The fisherman next to Jonah grinned wryly. "Well, I did a bit more than kiss her, but I'm relieved it didn't go any further than that. Though I wasn't at the time. But same thing, I didn't want to be the odd man out. Now I'm just glad not to be the odd man in." He flicked a twig in Jonah's direction. "We can't all be saints like Jonah here."

Saint Jonah was frozen. His breathing was shallow as, with what felt like great effort, he looked down the collection of fishermen lounged along the bank to one who hadn't spoken yet. The one who'd inadvertently shown Jonah that, though he'd thought his relationship with Lydia had been real, he'd just been used, one of many, played for a fool.

He remembered it clearly. He'd been so excited to see her at the frolic the day after they'd… The day after he'd broken his vows with her. But no matter how he tried to get close enough to be with her—to share a private smile, a covert touch—she'd evaded him. He'd finally caught a glimpse of her far down a row of buggies parked for the event. When she'd disappeared into one, he'd smiled and headed in that direction. Reaching the buggy and sliding open the door, he'd discovered it hadn't been him she'd been planning to meet.

She was already in the back, her arms around another man. At the sight of him, she'd closed her eyes and returned to avidly kissing the one she was with. Stunned, Jonah had backed away from the buggy, too numb, too shocked to even close the door. He'd been several buggies away before he realized, from the interior of the conveyance, whose it was. It'd been after

Lydia had left for Pennsylvania before he was no longer stilted with the one who'd once been a good friend.

Jonah sat up, his heart thumping, thumping, thumping, when that young man spoke.

"She all but pulled me into my buggy one time. Things were going great. I could certainly understand how she'd gotten her reputation. When all of a sudden, she burst into tears. Which certainly put a damper on things. She was crying so hard, I thought she was going to flood the back of the buggy. Needless to say, I didn't get what I thought everyone else was getting. But I wasn't going to admit that to you fellows either."

Jonah stared out over the pond, his hands fisted in the grass, the pole forgotten beside him.

One by one, all the young men in attendance admitted they'd exaggerated their exploits regarding Lydia.

"She must've been with someone. Maybe from another district? Why them and not us?"

Why indeed? Jonah rubbed a hand over the back of his neck. Why had she been with him when she hadn't with everyone else as he'd assumed? As everyone had assumed? As she'd said herself. Why was he different? Because she'd really cared for him? If so, why had she made sure he thought she'd raced to someone else right after being with him?

If these guys hadn't done what was rumored, did that mean others—ones not fishing today—who'd also hinted they'd been with her, hadn't either?

The rod beside him jerked in the grass. Jonah automatically closed his fingers around the cork grip. Talking ceased a moment at the *whirl* and *click* as the line ran out.

"Hey, you got a bite."

"Aren't you going to reel it in?"

"Come on, Jonah. Maybe it's a whale." The commenter snickered at his own joke.

"We might've been exaggerating our success with Lydia, but the only tales Jonah has to tell are fish stories," quipped another.

Jonah smiled stiffly at their ribbing as he reeled in the line, with little care if he caught anything. The outing had been very revealing. His mind elsewhere, he automatically responded to the give-and-take tug on the rod. He liked a puzzle, but Lydia was a growing conundrum.

If she hasn't been with any others as everyone assumes, why did she tell me I'm not Caleb's father? Or is that a lie too?

Chapter Eleven

Sighing, Lydia watched her *daed*'s buggy as it diminished into a black dot in the distance. Before he'd left, she'd assured him she would be all right. He'd assured her he'd be back in an hour. With the widow. And her family. She'd learned that the woman her father was courting did indeed have at least two unmarried daughters around her age. Ones who would conceivably move in when the widow did, although the prospective date of that occurrence may have been pushed back a bit.

Her lips twitched as she hitched Caleb onto her hip and the small bag for him that she'd kept with her onto her shoulder. Her minister father could hardly propose in the near term to the respectable widow, with the upcoming kneeling confession and possible shunning of his hussy daughter who was still living in his house. One who wouldn't tell, and some said, didn't even know who, the child's father was. Factors that were the antithesis to the faith, family and community bedrocks of Amish life.

It'd taken some convincing before she'd come today. To face what she knew was being said. It was one thing for folks to assume she was graciously taking care of a deceased relative's son. It was another to have it known that she was an unwed mother. It wasn't like she wasn't used to gossip. It was just that she'd always directed it away from herself. Now Lydia was sure she was so much the primary topic of discussions that she might as well paint the news on the side of the tallest silo in the district, much like the *Englisch* used billboards.

Perhaps sensing her unease, Caleb grasped one of her dangling prayer *kapp* ribbons and began to gnaw on it. Lydia didn't bother to retrieve it. Given an opportunity, she might've done something similar herself. Eyeing the nearby orchard, she suppressed the urge to hide amongst the trees until the event was over, but as it was a cider frolic, the orchard would be an area where many strolled today, including those who used the occasion to couple up. As assuredly, Rebecca and Jonah would. Her stomach hollowed at the thought.

Other than watching him arrive and depart from the farm, and hearing the sounds of construction through the securely closed door to the mudroom, she hadn't seen, nor spoken with Jonah since he stalked out of the kitchen three days ago. Every night after he'd left, she'd wandered through the addition, her chest tightening over the speed of progression. Progression which would precipitate his departure and the widow and family's arrival. Both events cause of little cheer. But if she cared for him at all, she shouldn't have him; she couldn't have him.

With another sigh, she pressed a kiss against Caleb's wispy hair. "Are you ready? We might as well go. It's either face them here, or tomorrow at church." With straightened shoulders and a purposeful stride through the closely cropped hayfield that was now repurposed as a parking area, Lydia headed for the neatly painted white buildings and the growing collection of plainly garbed folks weaving in and out of them.

To her relief, the first one she encountered was Rachel Raber, who along with Ben was lifting the twins down from their buggy. After settling a toddler on her own hip, Rachel sent a smile in her direction. "Lydia, I'm so glad you came."

For the moment, so was Lydia as she returned the smile. She joined the couple as they converged on the gathering, greeting others along the way. Though she felt some following gazes when they'd passed, since she was with the Rabers it was difficult for the rest to ignore her, even if they wanted to. With a wry smile, Lydia noted that the women who'd greeted them graciously were ones who'd more likely been subjects of her previous gossip, while the ones who viewed her coolly were the women who'd been avid listeners when she'd spread the rumors.

With the Rabers, she ambled up to where the press was running, the tart scent of apples evident from either the pulverizer that was crushing the apples as folks tossed them in a few at a time or from where the screw cranked the press plate down, forcing the juice from the mashed apples through the barreled cider press. Caleb pointed a tiny finger to where the amber liquid trickled from the funnel into containers.

"*Ja*. That's what it ends up like." Lydia picked up an apple from a nearby basket. "And this is what it starts out like. Shall we go pick some ourselves?" Determining she wouldn't mind hiding out in the trees after all, she decided the bubbles Caleb blew were an agreement to her decision. Setting the apple down and grabbing one of the available pails, Lydia waved to Rachel and, receiving a return one from her and a surprising nod from Ben, left what felt like the security of their company and headed toward the orchard. As she made her way, she passed others returning from the rows of small trees, carrying pails or baskets of the fruit. Most greeted her and Caleb with a nod or a smile, although some looked right through her and others glanced in her direction before making a hasty whisper to a companion.

Her own smile faltered with those encounters. She worked her way to a quiet part in the farther reaches of the orchard. Setting Caleb on the soft grass and propping his bag against a nearby tree trunk, she began picking windfall apples—not pretty, but still good for cider—from the ground around him. Caleb tried to help, or alternatively hinder, depending on whether he was putting apples, or other things, into the bucket at the moment or taking them out.

"If it takes thirty to forty apples to make a gallon of cider, with your help, we'll be lucky to get a cup full." Lydia didn't mind. She had come, something she hadn't really wanted to do, yet she was away from the crowd. Caleb could unload the bucket all he wanted. In fact…she rummaged through the bag until she found the small safety knife she'd tucked in it earlier. Selecting one of the better apples, she sat down and leaned against the tree's trunk to slice it into small sections for the boy, which Caleb crawled over and took with eager fingers.

"Do you think we can just hang out here all day? This way we can avoid everyone we don't want to see, which, unfortunately, is a long list, starting with Jonah." Sighing at the name, Lydia's chipper tone faltered for a moment. "There's plenty to eat, if you don't mind a limited diet, and I can manage—" she murmured as she glanced in the bag "— three diaper changes. Oh, you're giving me your cross-eyed look again. Does that mean you agree, or disagree?" One of the boy's eyes was directed at her, while the other appeared to be pointing toward his nose. Lydia frowned. She'd been seeing the look with more and more frequency. Was this normal for babies, or was it something she should be worried about?

The nearby snap of a twig, followed by a muffled weeping, startled her. Clutching Caleb closer, she craned her neck around the apple tree's trunk.

A solitary young woman was walking along the grassy avenue between the rows of trees behind Lydia. Her blond head was lowered as she dabbed away tears with the backs of her hands. Lydia ducked back around her tree trunk. Should she let the woman know she wasn't alone? Maybe the girl had been seeking solitude, like Lydia had. She was obviously unhappy.

Was it better to be unhappy alone, or with someone?

Lydia grimaced. She'd prefer to leave the blonde to her own devices, the same as she'd prefer her own privacy, but she recalled the unexpected comfort last week of Rachel's company. As she was drawing in a breath to announce her presence, Caleb beat her to it.

"Mamamama!"

Lydia poked her head back around the tree trunk to meet the young woman's startled gaze. "I'm afraid he's not very *gut* at Hide and Go Seek. Not that we were trying to hide," she hastened to clarify. "But if it was peace you were seeking, the atmosphere is lovely, but our company may be a little loud."

"Bababababa," Caleb interrupted her.

Rolling her eyes, Lydia added, "And unpredictable."

The woman dashed her hands across her

face again. Lydia didn't know her. She'd seen her sometime before, but she couldn't recall where. Though obviously distressed, the woman's tears hadn't ravaged her face. She was one of those women who wept prettily. Lydia used to envy those women. She'd envied a lot of women for a lot of reasons. Now she patted the ground beside her and offered an apple slice. "I didn't want to come today. But I felt it would be easier to face things today, than to wait and face them tomorrow."

After a brief hesitation, the blonde came over to gracefully sit and lean against the trunk beside Lydia. "I don't know if I could face anyone right now." Her breath hiccupped, "And I might not have to too much longer if I lose my job."

Wincing in sympathy, Lydia handed her the apple slice. "I'm sorry to hear that." She worried her lip. What would a "friend" do? What would she want now if she was upset and with someone she considered a "friend"?

"Do you want to…talk about it?"

"Talk is what's gotten me into trouble in the first place." The young woman's tears resumed. "Not my talk, but the talk of others." She sniffed. "They're saying I did something I didn't do. And now the school board may fire me over it."

Lydia exhaled to the extent that her lungs seemed empty of air. So this was Grace Kauffman, the schoolteacher, who, though an influencer of the district's children and a baptized member of the church, was supposedly attending *Englisch* parties. Even in her meager outings in the community, Lydia had heard the rumors and knew the girl's concerns were justified. As a spiritual leader, her minister father had even briefly discussed it with a school board member when he'd dropped her and Caleb off this morning.

For a moment, the confrontation of such grief resulting from gossip resurrected memories that were never far from the surface. Lydia squeezed her eyes shut against unwanted visions and recalled anguish. She panted shallowly as they played behind her closed eyes. Inhaling deeply through her nose, she drew in the scent of the ripened apples, of Caleb's sweet baby smell, heard the quiet drone of bees attracted by the ripened fruit and the distant murmur of voices. A previous perpetuator of gossip, she'd closed herself off to thoughts of the victim. She'd convinced herself that sharing rumors made her feel better about herself. At least she wasn't the subject. She had some semblance of control in the telling, something she didn't have in other aspects of her life.

But that'd changed on a dark night in Pennsylvania. Granted, she'd apologized to Rachel, but she was only one person out of numerous and it was over a year after the gossip she shared had swirled around the young woman. What about the others? Rachel was now securely established in her life. Maybe she had been then as well, but whether she had been or not didn't diminish Lydia's wrongdoing. What about those who hadn't been? Whose lives might've been irreparably changed in some way by what had been said?

Lydia didn't know what to say. Opening her eyes, she stared numbly down at the partial apple in her hand before she began to cut additional slices from it, handing them to Caleb and her new companion. Juice dribbled down Caleb's chin as he gnawed on the fruit.

The young woman regarded him with a smile. "He's sweet. Is he yours?"

"Ja." Lydia blotted Caleb's chin with a cloth from the bag. This, at least, was a subject she could now speak on without remorse. "He is." She was glad to finally and fully claim him. She'd felt shame, and fear about her situation, particularly at first. But once Caleb had arrived, all she felt was love. For him, and for her cousin Mary, who, with her support, had made it possible for Lydia to keep her son.

The rumors that were churning about her were true, or at least had some reasonable semblance of validity. She'd done what she'd done. And to some minds, had tried to hide it. But, looking into Grace's eyes, Lydia didn't doubt that this young woman was telling the truth.

"What are you going to do?"

Grace shook her head. "I don't know."

Instead of eating the apple slice, Grace broke it into small pieces which she pitched aside. Lydia made a mental note to ensure Caleb didn't crawl into that area later to find and try to consume the disposed morsels.

"If I'm fired, I suppose I'll have to go back home to Iowa, but I like it here in Miller's Creek and," Grace's chin quivered, "my return will be hard to explain, when I don't understand it myself."

"It is a *gut* community, though it might not seem so to you right now."

Grace gave her a tentative smile. "Are you from here? I don't recall meeting you before."

"I was gone for a year. I returned to some…" she bounced her knee a few times to a jounced Caleb's delight, "…talk regarding me as well."

After an initial furrowed brow, Grace's eyes widened. "Oh, you're…"

"*Ja.* That's me."

Following a brief study of Lydia's bland expression, the young woman's smile expanded. "I'm Grace Kauffman. I'm the schooltea—" she caught herself. "Well, for the meantime, I'm the schoolteacher here."

"It is my pleasure to meet you, Grace." Lydia hesitated, then added facetiously, "I've heard about you."

Grace looked momentarily startled, before she snorted—another thing she did delicately—with laughter. "I've heard about you too… Lydia?"

They shared a commiserating glance before, having spied a cricket, Caleb lunged off Lydia's lap to go in pursuit. She captured him before he caught the insect.

"I suppose we should see if anyone other than us provided enough apples to make ample cider to share." Rising to her feet, Lydia settled her son on her hip and entertained him by picking some of the low-hanging apples to put in her bucket before she turned to Grace. "Are you ready?"

With a deep breath and a faint nod, the young woman rose to her feet and brushed off the back of her dress. "As you said, better today than tomorrow."

Plucking a few apples herself to add to the

bucket, Grace took charge of it while Lydia snagged Caleb's bag from the base of the tree. Side by side, they sauntered back through the trees, tacitly slowing their strides as they began to encounter other people. Glancing at the pale but resolute profile beside her, Lydia gave a slight shake of her head. She was discovering friends in the strangest places.

As they emerged from the orchard, someone called Grace's name. Giving the schoolteacher a reassuring smile, Lydia waved her off. Although there were several other folks around, for a moment, Lydia felt oddly deserted when Grace walked away, even though she had encouraged her. Switching Caleb to her other arm, Lydia continued toward where the apple press was still in use before drawing to an abrupt halt when she recognized the women in her direct path. A quick glance around told her it was too late to again find refuge amongst the apple trees.

With a thudding heart, she looked ahead to watch the approach of the widow and her two daughters.

Chapter Twelve

A quick glance around revealed no sign of her father. Lydia had never been introduced to the trio. Just because she knew who they were, didn't mean they would recognize her. Perhaps she could pass right by them. Dredging up a noncommittal smile, Lydia tore her gaze from the widow's to focus past the woman's right shoulder. To her chagrin, it then landed on Jonah, helping a laughing Rebecca fill a jug of cider as it funneled from the press, a sight that caused a further tightening in her stomach.

"Lydia?"

Too late. The smile, though stiff, stayed pinned to Lydia's lips as she slid her attention back to the pleasant-faced, graying-haired woman. *"Ja?"*

The widow's friendly expression didn't

dim. In fact, it looked quite welcoming. But Lydia knew appearances could be deceiving. Look how her *daed* had been fooled enough to marry her *mamm*.

The woman's eyes crinkled with her smile. "I hope I'm not being too bold. Your father pointed you out at the auction last week, though we were too far away to say hello. And this must be Caleb." Extending a hand toward the boy, the widow pulled it back when Caleb shrank against Lydia's shoulder. "They get a little shy at this age, don't they?"

Lydia didn't have an answer for that. Caleb hadn't shrunk away from Grace. But that'd been under a quiet apple tree and not confronting three strangers when the mother who held him was shaking like a leaf.

"Your father has spoken of you."

I'm sure he has. Lydia didn't have an answer to that either. Given the recent events, what had her father said?

Though the woman's pleasant countenance never faltered, she glanced around. "Henry was here just a moment ago. Perhaps I should've left the introductions to him, but I saw you and was excited to meet. Forgive me. Though he has spoken to us about you, he may not have mentioned anything about us to you. I'm

Edna, and these are my daughters, Mary Ann and Susie."

The women she gestured to, close to Lydia's own age, had apparently heard Lydia spoken of before as well, and not necessarily just from her father. They both regarded Lydia with suspicious gazes mirroring the one she returned to them.

The quartet awkwardly regarded each other and might have for some time if her *daed* hadn't appeared at the widow's elbow. Glancing between Lydia and the older woman, he rubbed his hands together. "So, you've met?"

The echo of *jas* assured him that they had. The silence following indicated they didn't have much to add beyond that. With a range of smiles, the widow's being the most genuine, they all considered each other until Henry cleared his throat.

"I've been looking forward to the taste of cider. Shall we go pick some apples to add to the process?"

The widow and her daughters hastened to agree that would be a *gut* idea. Maybe they just figured it would be a *gut* idea to put some space between them all?

As they turned in the direction of the grove of trees, she stayed put. "Caleb and I just came from the orchard. If you don't mind that we don't join you?"

They apparently didn't mind, as they left quickly enough. Maybe it was wrong not to go. Maybe she should've joined them and in doing so, the awkwardness would've eventually dissipated. Maybe the widow—Edna— was as kind as she appeared. Getting to know her better may've helped make a more accurate determination. Although, even on short acquaintance it was difficult to *really* know someone. Some folks had thought her *mamm* had been a pleasant woman. They hadn't had to live with her. Maybe it wasn't fair to assume her *daed* wouldn't choose wisely for a life mate the second time. But look how he'd done on the first?

Would he be disappointed in her because she hadn't made more of an effort to get to know his new family? Lydia snorted softly. Given her current circumstances, it was hard to imagine her father being any more disappointed in her than he already was. So disappointed he'd told everyone about her situation? The news that she had a child but no husband had gotten out awfully fast.

She pressed a hand against her stomach when she found herself again facing Jonah and Rebecca, though the couple had moved on to carrying some of the apple pulp from the press to where the mashed fruit was being collected to later be distributed as livestock feed. Maybe she should've joined her *daed* and future family since, uncomfortable as that'd been, at least they would've been a barrier to others here.

Maybe she should've followed her instincts not to come today in the first place.

Jonah dumped his bucket of pulp and reached out for the one Rebecca held. His thoughts were as convoluted as the tangled peelings tumbling into the large barrel. Though he wasn't looking in her direction, he knew within a few feet of where Lydia stood—with the child who could quite possibly be his. His senses had thrummed like they were hooked to a powerful generator even before he'd seen her emerge from the trees with Grace.

Though he longed to challenge her regarding what he'd learned this morning, he kept his distance. He was here with Rachel. He couldn't approach Lydia about this topic with the woman he was presumably walking out with by his side. And what was he to say anyway?

The handle of the empty bucket gripped in a tense fist, Jonah stared into the barrel of mangled apples. Women were complicated. Two women were more complicated and troublesome than forty cantankerous cows.

Why had Lydia lied to him about other men? Not that her history always had a particularly close relationship with the truth, but about something like that, wouldn't she have preferred that he see her in a better light instead of the worst one possible? She'd encouraged all the lies about herself, by her words and actions. Why would someone do that? Did not the *Biewel* say in Proverbs that "a good name is rather to be chosen than great riches"? Jonah strove very hard to make sure his name, his father's name, maintained a good reputation. Why would Lydia intentionally sully hers?

He'd been numb when he'd abruptly left the pond this morning. Having automatically reeled in the large bass on his line, he'd equally unwittingly freed it from the hook and tossed it back into the water, to a chorus of protests from his fellow fishermen.

If the crowd she'd supposedly been with had, in truth, dwindled to a few, if any, was Caleb—regardless of what Lydia claimed— his son? Jonah inhaled sharply. Even in the outdoors, it didn't seem like he could draw in enough air at the thought.

His senses were still humming like a disturbed bee hive. Was it anger that burned through him? Not at being a father—that prospect filled him more with a tentative joy than displeasure—but at Lydia, for denying him that right? Was it anger at the turmoil she'd caused him? Continually caused him? Even before she'd denied his parentage, he'd been so disappointed to have been suckered in again, thinking she was different, only to discover at the auction that she hadn't really changed, that he'd avoided her, unwilling to continually face her lies.

But if her loose reputation was all lies, what was real? That she'd actually cared for him? Or was that just his wishful thinking?

Jonah's mouth twitched. He claimed to be a problem solver. He'd never faced a bigger or more impacting one to his life than this. He scrubbed a hand over his face, the scent of apples on it teasing his nostrils. The way he'd been handling his mistrust with Lydia obviously hadn't been effective. Would another confrontation with her make a difference? He shot a glance at Lydia, who was pointedly looking in a different direction.

Probably not.

As she was looking away, from across the short distance, Jonah took a moment to study the boy she held, seeking any sign of himself in the child. Caleb's hair, what there was of it, was not red like his mother's but darker. *Like his.* But also, like Henry's hair before it'd grayed.

Grimacing, Jonah turned from the barrel to find Rebecca watching him. Another grimace almost rippled over his face. He'd arranged with Rebecca to meet up at the frolic before this morning's fishing trip. When Lydia had proven at the auction that she hadn't changed, and particularly following her flat-out denial that he was Caleb's father, he'd determined it was time he should take the relationship with Rebecca to a deeper level. To finally get serious about a future with her. Fall was, traditionally, the time young Amish couples had the bishop or deacon announce the couple's intentions in church, followed by their wedding taking place a few weeks later.

That prospect, one he'd been unable to get truly excited about though he did care for Rebecca, had definitely changed. There was no way, now that he knew there was a possibility he might be Caleb's father, of continuing a relationship with Rebecca. Not when he might have a son he'd need to—wanted to—claim along with the boy's mother. Swallowing something that tasted suspiciously like guilt, he dropped his gaze. It wasn't fair to

Rebecca. He'd have to end it. And soon. But he didn't want to hurt her either. He almost flinched when her shoulder brushed his as they carried their empty buckets back to the cider press.

Forty? *Ach*, he'd take eighty cantankerous cows and an indecisive construction customer rather than deal with two women.

The reins were growing damp under Jonah's sweaty palms. How did one go about breaking up with a girl? At least Lydia had spared him that. When he'd found her in the arms of another man, that'd been it; there'd been no need for any further discussion. He looked over at Rebecca. She hadn't seemed surprised when, as the frolic was winding down, he'd asked to take her home. She hadn't seemed happy about the invitation either. She looked at him, then at the Troyer buggy which was just turning out of the lane.

His knee started bouncing. Rebecca glanced at it from where she was sitting, much farther over on the seat than where she usually sat when they'd ridden in the buggy alone together. Scowling, she returned her attention to the road ahead.

"You might as well get it over with."

His horse threw his head up when Jonah's hands inadvertently tightened on the reins.

"I know why you asked to take me home today. I won't say that I'm not disappointed, because I am. But I'm also not surprised. I see where your gaze keeps going. I'm not sure what's going on there. But something is."

Jonah rubbed a hand over the back of his neck. He wasn't sure what was going on there either. *Ach*, at least she'd broached the topic so he didn't have to, but he still wasn't sure how to continue the conversation. "I do care for you, Rebecca, but…"

"It's never *gut* to use *but* in a sentence like that. You're going to say some version of 'but not enough,' or like they say in the *Englisch* magazines, 'it's not you—it's me.'" Rebecca crossed her arms over her chest. "It is you, Jonah. I hope you figure out for yourself whatever it is that's going on. But don't ask me to wait while you do so."

That hadn't been what he'd been going to say, but while it didn't use the exact words he would have, it expressed his thoughts. Maybe he needed to read *Englisch* magazines for this type of thing. Better yet, avoid this type of thing altogether. "I won't ask you to wait—it wouldn't be the right thing to do."

Rebecca sighed and shook her head. "And

you always do the right thing, don't you, Jonah."

Heat crept up his face. No. He'd done far from the right thing. He certainly hadn't fallen for the right girl. As a wife, Rebecca would probably suit him far better than Lydia would. The right thing? Jonah wasn't even sure what it was at the moment. But he was going to figure it out. He just didn't know yet how. He did know this: until he sorted things out with Lydia, he wasn't good for anyone else.

Chapter Thirteen

After the church service, Lydia had handed Caleb off to one of the young girls who were minding the little ones under a large maple tree in the yard and went to help in the kitchen as she had the previous church Sunday. Volunteering to wash the returning plates and silverware, she appreciated the opportunity to keep her back to the room. And its occupants.

She'd been greeted with more smiles than she'd expected, but like the last service the day after her return two weeks ago, she knew glances had been cast her way. Particularly when it was announced that a Members' Meeting would be held after the next Sunday worship service. Before Lydia had dropped her gaze to Caleb, sitting on her lap, she'd noted that the speculative attention not directed at her was focused on the schoolteacher, Grace, sitting white-faced on an adjoining bench.

A kneeling confession before the congregation and a possible *ban*. Would it be any worse than being outnumbered by strangers living in her own home? Her *daed* had taken the widow and her daughters to their residence yesterday before returning to pick her and Caleb up. Their own ride home had been quiet. Though he didn't say it, Lydia could tell by his behavior that he was disappointed she hadn't made more of an effort to get to know the women.

Would a short acquaintance be enough to trust that the widow wouldn't be any different than her mother? Maybe…maybe it would be best if she returned to Pennsylvania. She'd longed to come home, but it was becoming a home much different than she'd expected. It might be better for all if she left. Her departure would make an easier transition for her *daed*'s new family to move in, and later, or maybe even before, Jacob's wife.

Lydia sighed. And it would be better for Jonah. Though she'd tried to avoid looking at him in church this morning, it seemed whenever she'd looked up, it was to meet his troubled gaze. One that knotted her stomach. She ached at having hurt him, but she couldn't let him think that he was Caleb's father. Couldn't let him, or herself, think they might have a future.

At least he wouldn't be venturing into the kitchen while they were cleaning up after the Sunday meal. And neither would the widow and her daughters, as they would be attending their own district's service. Lydia had never thought that a sink full of dishes could be a haven.

She was arms deep in sudsy water when the tenor of conversation behind her changed. The cheerful chatter hadn't ceased, but had dimmed slightly. Looking over her shoulder, she saw Grace Kauffman enter the kitchen at the side of another woman who'd moved into Miller's Creek in the year Lydia had been gone.

Miriam Raber had been Miriam Schrock when she'd first arrived in the area. Though Lydia had learned who she was, she hadn't been introduced to the woman, which was fine with her. It might prove a little embarrassing, depending on how much Miriam had talked with her siblings because at different times, Lydia had made a play for all three Schrock brothers, with no success. Well, she'd kissed Samuel, but it hadn't taken much of an effort for a young woman to get Samuel Schrock to kiss her before he'd met and married Gail. The only reason she hadn't flirted heavily with Aaron, Miriam's new husband, was because he'd been walking out with Rachel up until the time he'd left for the *Englisch* over a year ago and hadn't returned prior to Lydia's departure for Pennsylvania. *Nee*, Miriam Raber had no reason to want to pursue a friendship with her.

Lydia would've turned back around if she hadn't seen Grace's face pale at the diminished conversations upon her arrival and an assessing glance or two sent in her direction.

Under the bubbles, her hands clenched on the silverware, the prongs of a few forks poking into her palms. She'd entered the kitchen earlier to the same looks, the same subtle change in the buzz of conversation. While the far majority of the community had been kind, there were a few who thrived on gossip. Due to her own guilt, the weight of their reproach was amplified. Still, she'd ignored it and gotten to work. She didn't blame them for talking. The community had rules for a purpose. Bylaws that members agreed to when they were baptized into the church. To break them brought consequences. She'd broken them. But all was forgiven if one confessed to the sin. The process was important in helping maintain the church's purity.

What was being shared about Lydia by those who thrived on doing such things was true. But not what was being said about Grace. Grace, who should bear no guilt, but who still felt the pain as the target of gossip and whose life might be irrevocably changed over tales told out of hand. Another person devastated by talk…

Lydia's chest constricted. Shaking the water and suds off her hands, she turned to fully face those in the kitchen. Words were tumbling out before she was even aware of opening her mouth.

"Have you asked her if the gossip is true? I don't know Grace well, but she doesn't strike me as one who would betray the trust the community has given her regarding its children. Has anyone here actually seen her do anything that would suggest what you might've heard has any truth to it? Why don't you ask her instead of believing a rumor? Do you even know the rumor's source?"

A source that in all likelihood had been Lydia's own sister. Lucetta, who Lydia had been just like…before. Maybe still was. Maybe always would be. She swallowed against the bile rising at the back of her throat.

Faces, partially framed by various shades of hair neatly confined in prayer *kapps*, were all turned in her direction. The kitchen was silent. All talking had stopped. Even the faint murmur of conversation in the common room beyond the kitchen had ceased.

Heat raced up her neck. Lydia knew it was likely beet red next to the white ribbons of her *kapp*. Even her ears felt like they were burning. She fisted her hands to keep from tugging the edge of her *kapp* over them at the attention centered on her.

Longing to turn around or better yet, somehow escape the room, Lydia cleared her throat, and with a hoarse voice, continued. "Maybe it was just made up by someone who was envious of Grace."

She licked suddenly parched lips. "That's why I spread the rumors I did. To bring someone down because I didn't feel capable of rising to their level. If you're passing a rumor on, you're doing the same thing. We're more apt to judge the subject of gossip when maybe we should be judging the gossiper. Isn't gossiping a sin as well?"

Shaking, growing lightheaded, she leaned back against the sink for support and drew in a shuddering breath. "Regarding Caleb and I. *Ja*. I am his mother. Talk all you want about that. It's fact. But don't believe the unfounded rumors about Grace and spread them no further."

Pushing away from the sink, with downcast eyes and rubbery knees, she dodged her way around those in the kitchen until she made it to the door. Once outside, she headed for the large maple tree where she'd left Caleb with the other little ones. Scooping him up and grabbing his bag, she gave a strained smile of thanks to the young girls who'd been minding him before striding in the direction of the buggies.

She'd passed the first one before her pace slowed. What was she going to do now? Where was she going to go? Church Sundays extended well into the day. It was too far to walk home, at least while carrying Caleb. She'd come with her father and he wouldn't be leaving for hours yet. What was she to do? Nausea threatened at the prospect of having to return to the house for the remainder of the afternoon.

Her energy draining away like a floodgate had been opened, Lydia's pace slowed even further. Spying her *daed*'s buggy, she numbly angled in that direction, only to freeze at the call of her name from behind her. She stiffened. A man's voice. *Oh please, don't let it be Jonah. I couldn't bear to face him right now.*

Turning apprehensively, her rigid shoulders sagged at the sight of her brother Jacob leading his harnessed horse at the far end of the grassy aisle.

"Need a ride?"

"I… How did you know?"

"Miriam found me and said you might be wanting to go home. Not later, but now. For sure and certain, she can be persuasive when she wants to be." Though he smiled, Lydia was startled to see what looked like concern in his eyes. For her? Surely not.

"I would. *Denki.* Truly."

Leading the way to his buggy, he assisted her in getting a drowsy Caleb inside before hitching his horse up. A moment later, they were pulling onto the road. They traveled silently for a while, the only sounds the *clip-clop* of the horse's hooves, the clatter of the wheels and the occasional snuffle of Caleb asleep on her shoulder.

Lydia looked over at her unexpected rescuer. Though Jacob was her nearest brother in age, she'd never felt particularly close to him. Apparently feeling her attention, he glanced at her and raised an eyebrow.

"I'm sorry to have made you leave early. You probably wanted to stay, to visit and such."

He shrugged. "It's all right. I know a few guys from the next district over. I kind of, uh, wouldn't mind seeing if their afternoon activities and singings are any different than ours."

"Know a few guys?"

"*Ja*, and his sister." Jacob's smile was sheepish. "I mean, their sisters."

Lulled by the familiar traveling sounds, with a drowsing Caleb cuddled against her, the residue of tension from the disaster in the kitchen and her resultant embarrassment slowly seeped from Lydia. Careful to not disturb the boy, she pressed her hands to her now cool cheeks.

"Did you ever say something you...shouldn't have?" The question was rhetorical but to her surprise, after a brief considering frown, Jacob shook his head.

"*Nee*. I leave that to my sisters."

Her mouth sagged before Lydia realized that along with the comment, Jacob had winked at her. She supposed she should've been offended, but instead, an ember of connection flared at the retort. Was this a brotherly tease? It felt *gut*. She might not've enjoyed it growing up, but experiencing it now was a balm to her frayed senses.

Lydia gently rubbed a hand over Caleb's back, relishing his warm weight nestled against her. Maybe things could be different. She had no idea what the result of her outburst would be. Hopefully she could hide away at home and not face anyone until—she gave a gusty sigh—until she had to kneel in front of them all at the Members' Meeting in a few weeks.

She would confess her sin of fornication. Her lips slanted. *Ach*, if they wanted an additional confession on gossiping, she'd certainly already given them one, though she hadn't been kneeling at the time. Humiliating as the upcoming ordeal in front of the congregation would be, she *was* remorseful of her actions. She ran a light finger down Caleb's soft cheek to his lips that'd drifted open in his sleep. She truly regretted the gossiping and the fornication, but she couldn't regret her son.

Her heartbeat lurched into a cadence faster than the trotting horse as she sat up straight. Would they ask her to confess who Caleb's father was? She couldn't. If she did, Jonah would insist on marrying her. And if she didn't, would they all vote to ban her? That level of punishment needed the unanimous agreement of the members.

Though the ministers did try to work to keep private matters private, allowing a confidential free-will confession for those whose offenses were not public knowledge, Caleb was obvious evidence of her broken vows;

therefore a public confession was required. The structure of their community was based on *Gelassenheit*, an attitude of submission. Those who displayed contrition were quickly forgiven and returned to fellowship.

But wasn't the whole process of her public confessing to bring about her change? Didn't today, where instead of augmenting rumors, she'd sought to stop them, prove that she had changed? That she was capable of changing? Her breath came faster. And if she was capable of changing, did she still have to rule out the possibility of a life with Jonah? For a moment, she hugged the thought to herself. Just because her mother had been the way she was didn't mean Lydia had to be as well, did it? Wasn't the determination that her son would never know the unending criticism of her youth some evidence of transformation?

Hope, something so alien she struggled to recognize it, sparked to life.

But reality kept it from flaring. Those who showed contrition were forgiven and eagerly returned to the fold, but those who challenged authority faced harsher judgment. If she didn't admit her son's parentage now, they would expect her to do so after the six-week ban.

What if she couldn't change enough to suit

herself, to suit what she knew Jonah needed, deserved, by then? If she didn't confess Caleb's father then, she would be fully excommunicated.

Lydia dipped her chin at the heart-wrenching prospect. Her eyes squeezed shut. *Please, Gott, show me some sign that I am not like my mother. That I haven't inherited that destructive legacy. That change is indeed possible.*

Chapter Fourteen

Josiah gave Paul's shoulder a bump as he swung open the barn door to envelope them all with the smell particular to a dairy milk house. "I wouldn't be surprised if Jonah tried to breed the black spots out of our Holsteins if he could, figuring it'd make it easier to see all white cows in the dark during early morning milkings."

While his other two younger brothers snickered at Josiah's comment, Jonah was glad the darkness hid his own smile. He didn't mind their teasing, though he'd never let them know that. His *breider* might joke about Jonah's running debate with their father, but they'd embraced some of his suggestions, like the LED headlamps they all wore. Josiah flicked his on, illuminating the milk house's stainless steel wash tub and racks, the latter with numerous milk cans stored upside down in neat rows, their pristine covers beside them.

"Well, I suppose it would save us on batteries." Continuing through to the milking parlor, Harley turned on lanterns situated on beams throughout, adding further glow to the stanchions lining both sides of the cleaned concrete floor bordered by equally clean gutters. While kerosene lamps were used in some places of the house, no open flames were allowed in the barn.

"He'd probably try to develop a line of cows with taller legs so we could stand while milking and not waste time with the milking stools," quipped Paul as he traveled down the aisle in front of the stanchions, distributing hay and grain for the cows that would soon be parading into the parlor.

"Don't forget the cost savings of not having stools." Josiah carried a quartet of stainless steel pails in from the milk house.

Jonah grunted as he swung the top Dutch door on the far side of the parlor open to be greeted by several black-and-white bovine faces. "It just makes sense to breed for seventy pounds of milk a day per cow, even though Holsteins can produce more. By the time we manually milk our size herd, that's about all our hands can take. Especially for you slackers."

"Who're you calling a slacker?" Having staged the pails and disinfectant for his siblings, Josiah dodged flicking tails as the cows swarmed past him on their way to the stanchions.

"If the name fits…" The sound of milk hissing into pails already cut through the parlor. Jonah snagged a milking stool from a hook on the wall, collected his other items and perched on the one-legged device. Setting a pail under the cow, he automatically checked her feet to see if any needed treating. A cow that couldn't stand wasn't much good on a farm. Making quick work of the disinfectant used before and after milking that protected both cow and milk, he leaned his forehead against the Holstein's warm flank and began the work he'd done since he was big enough to contribute to the twice a day milkings.

Though he didn't participate, he listened to his brothers' continued bantering with a rueful smile. He'd miss this if he left the family business. Miss the peace of the barn. In a Wisconsin winter, there was nothing like stepping into its warm and cozy environment, redolent with the scent of clean hay and the particular homey aroma of the cows that were housed there that time of year. The comforting sound of cows lowing, the jesting of his brothers, the amused grunt of his *daed* when he'd join in the milking, all were music that soothed his soul.

How could he leave it? He didn't resent that Harley would inherit the farm. That was just the way it generally was for the Amish, with the assumption that when the older sons of a large family were mature, their father would still be farming. Jonah's gaze slid over to his youngest brother, diligently milking across the aisle. Though young, Harley was a hard worker, a fast learner and seemed passionate about the family business. He would be a *gut* steward for the farm. A farm not big enough to support much more than one family. If Jonah wanted to continue in the dairy business, he would need to figure out a way— with the agreement of those involved—to expand this one, or start his own. An expensive option.

Or just leave it and expand his carpentry operation. An occupation he enjoyed for different reasons.

After finishing up with that cow, he repeated the process with the next. His lips canted as he tipped momentarily before balancing his weight on the one-legged stool. Maybe Paul was onto something with breeding taller cows and eliminating the need for the stools. For every problem, there was generally a solution, even though it might take a while to get there.

He'd been thinking of problems and solutions during the three-hour church service yesterday. Solutions to his problems with women, both of whom he'd been facing across the rows of benches. One had avoided his gaze and, well, he hadn't been too keen himself on connecting with the other.

It would probably be a while before he and Rebecca were comfortable around each other again. The smallness—around twenty families, as was normal for most Amish districts—of their community would make it a bit awkward as they would run into each other frequently. He should probably avoid eating at the Dew Drop restaurant where she worked as a waitress in the meantime to avoid an "accidental" glass of water tipped in his lap. When he'd given her a ride home—and they'd broken off their relationship—their parting had been more than a little stiff.

But regarding the one avoiding his gaze... though his hands continued to work, Jonah leaned away from the cow. During the long second sermon, he'd come up with a path forward regarding Lydia. He wanted to confront her. Wanted to know the truth. Was Caleb his son? If so, why did she deny it? Beyond that, could he trust her? And if she had been lying—and she was lying about something—why should he want to?

Too many friends' denials refuted some of her claims about how she'd shared herself. Both couldn't be true. So if she had been lying about the other, then Caleb was his son. And he would marry his son's mother to make a family. Besides—Jonah's hands paused in their automatic rhythm; the cow swished her tail at the delay—he cared for her. He missed their talks. There was just something about Lydia that called to him. But like the spooked creature he'd once compared her to, before you could work with it in a team, before you could even really approach the creature, you had to gain trust. Be around, but give space. Let the wary one get comfortable around you. Be nonthreatening. He would confront Lydia by not confronting her.

And once he got close to her, then he'd find out the truth.

Lydia looked over from where she was securing a damp towel to the clothesline when the *clip-clop* of hooves slowed and turned into the lane instead of continuing by on the blacktop. Glancing down, she checked where Caleb was patting the wet clothes in the basket with one hand while the other gripped the edge of the wicker container. Assured of his security, she lifted her gaze, shading it with one hand to see who the unexpected arrival might be. A grimace flickered across her face when she identified the driver.

Lydia hung three more dish towels by the time her sister exited the buggy and hitched her horse to the post. She thought Lucetta had arrived alone until her two nieces perched a wary moment at the buggy's open door before cautiously descending down the steps. Hands pausing on the recently pinned towel, Lydia's heart clenched as four-year-old Malinda turned to assist her two-year-old sister. The petite pair didn't get a backward glance from Lucetta as her sister crossed the yard toward the clothesline.

When the girls got closer, Fannie broke into a run to reach Lydia and hug her leg. Instantly kneeling, Lydia gave her a quick hug in return and set her up at the edge of the wicker basket along with Caleb, entertaining them by tossing several wooden clothes pins amongst the remaining clothes for them to find. Malinda crept up beside her to silently watch.

"Would you like to help?" Lydia smiled at her.

The girl timidly nodded.

"You'd help me a whole lot if you'd hand me a couple of clothespins for every item I grab."

The girl's thin face creased in a small smile and she nimbly fished a few pins from the basket and put them in Lydia's outreached hand.

Lucetta glanced at the byplay without interest. "I came to say goodbye."

"What?" A pair of her *daed*'s pants dropped from her fingers with a damp *thwack* on the ground. Malinda hastily rescued the apparel and held it up by one leg. Taller than she was, the pants dangled from her dainty fingers, leaving the majority of the garment to trail in the short grass. Her mind whirling, Lydia numbly reached for the item and pinned it to the clothesline. The line and attached wash drooped as Lydia curled her hands around the cool wire and sagged against it.

"Where are you going?" Were they moving to another district? Though not necessarily prosperous, her brother-in-law seemed to be holding his own on his small farm, but perhaps he'd decided to sell out here for a profit and try somewhere else where land was cheaper. New Amish settlements were being established all the time. Peter didn't have any other family in their district, having inherited the farm from a bachelor uncle, so he didn't have strong ties to the community.

Lydia narrowed her eyes at her sister. Lucetta was simmering with excitement. Maybe the couple had patched up their situation, Peter had moved back in from the *daadi haus* and they'd determined to make a new start somewhere else. Lydia hoped so for the girls' sake. One hand dropped to rest on Malinda's shoulder. She would miss them. Her chest tightened as the little girl looked up at her with solemn eyes. *She would worry for them.*

"If you don't know, you can't tell." Lydia's gaze flew to her sister's face in time to catch Lucetta's smirk.

"What?" Lydia echoed from before. Her hand on the wire sagged farther, dragging the line down and causing the bottom of her *daed*'s pants to touch the ground. Something cool brushed against the hand she'd placed on Malinda's shoulder. Glancing down, Lydia expected to see a fluttering piece of laundry, instead finding small fingers grasping what they could of hers. Adjusting her grip, Lydia curled her palm protectively around Malinda's miniature hand.

"I met a man. An *Englisch* one. He's leaving the area and I'm going with him."

Lydia's knees buckled until her one-handed grip on the clothesline was the only thing holding her up. That and the trusting clasp of the little one beside her.

"What about the girls?" She whispered the question through numb lips.

Lucetta shrugged a dismissive shoulder. "They'll stay with their father. I'm not taking them with me. I've been taking care of a household and kids, including you, since I wasn't much more than her age." She nodded to where Lydia could feel Malinda pressed against her hip, keeping her partially blocked from her mother's view. "I want a break. I want to be free from responsibilities for once in my life. I'm only twenty-two years old." She plucked at the skirt of her plain dress as if it offended her. "I want to be pretty. I want to have fun."

Lydia struggled to get her breath. Her sister was voicing desires opposite of the foundations of their faith. Humbleness, submission, hard work, responsibility. Abiding in *Gott's* laws. Values Lydia believed in, though she hadn't always upheld them.

"But you've been baptized into the church. If you leave, you'll be excommunicated. Think about what that would do to *Daed* in his role as minister."

"It doesn't matter if I'm not coming back."

"You made vows before *Gott*. You made them to your husband." Lydia shook her head in bewilderment. "Marriage is for life. Even if you leave, Peter can never remarry as long as you're alive."

"That's not much of a loss for anyone. He's a pretty poor example of a husband."

"How can you say that? Peter is a *gut* man. A hard worker. How can you do this to him when you used him to get out of the house?" Did she even know this woman who was her sister?

Lucetta's lips twisted into an expression that was far from her goal of being pretty. "How many men did you use in your attempts to get out of the house?" Her gaze dropped to Caleb, who was looking between the two women with wide, uncertain eyes. "I'd say I did a better job getting out with my one than you did with your many. So many you couldn't even put an identity on who his father is, to at least get the man, some man, to marry you."

"I know exactly who Caleb's father is. I love him." Lydia wanted to double over and howl in her anguish. This tainted behavior was her ilk, her lot in life. And because of it, there was no hope for a future with Jonah. Releasing the wire, she pressed her hand against her stomach to control the ache. "That's the reason I'll never marry him. Because I'm afraid I'll end up like our mother. Or like you. And I won't tie him to that kind of life."

"My, my, aren't you the noble one." Lucetta propped her hands on her hips. "Well, I don't know why I bothered coming over. I thought of any of my family, at least you'd understand. You have a worse reputation than I do. Thanks, by the way, for being so newsworthy—you took the attention away from my actions. Come on, girls." Lucetta jerked her head toward the buggy.

Malinda's tiny-fingered grip tightened on her hand. Lydia's heart ached for the little one. "When are you leaving?"

"Another thing I'm not going to tell. What, you want to go share the news? Fuel your gossip? Oh, I forgot. You don't share gossip anymore. Only be the subject of it. *Ja*, I heard about yesterday. You can make all the noise you want about changing, but I know you. You'll never be anything other than what you are. The apple, especially if it's a rotten one, never falls far from the tree."

Tears ran in hot trails down Lydia's face. Malinda slowly released her hand and went to take her little sister's. On choppy strides, they crossed the yard, Fannie looking back once. When they reached the buggy, Lucetta waited to lift the two-year-old in. While Malinda laboriously ascended the steps by herself, Lucetta freed the horse from the post and climbed into the buggy. The door slammed shut. Jerking its head at the rough tug on the bit, the horse wheeled and lunged down the lane.

Caleb started crying, his green eyes shimmering in tears as he reached his arms up to Lydia. Instead of picking him up, she sank to the ground beside him and gathered him to her, needing his comfort as much as he needed hers.

She'd asked *Gott* to show her she wasn't like her mother. Apparently, this was His answer.

Chapter Fifteen

"Begin as you mean to go on." Jonah couldn't recall where he'd heard the advice, but it seemed fitting for this situation. He meant to reconnect with Lydia. To regain her trust. To see if there would be a reason to regain his in her. That meant spending time together, starting with sharing meals together again. If she didn't throw him out. Or poison him.

Sliding his sweating palms down the front of his pants, he drew in a fortifying breath and rapped on the door, the resulting reverberation through the concrete-floored mudroom sounding more confident than he felt. All was silent for the span of several heartbeats. Did Lydia not hear him? It was noon. She'd usually be in the kitchen this time of day. He knocked again. This time, tipping his ear closer to the door, he detected a muffled response. Had it been "come in," "go away" or something in between?

"Begin as you mean to go on." Going on, or even beginning, meant interpreting it as the former. Turning the handle, Jonah opened the door a crack. When no one was in his line of sight, he pushed it wider to reveal Lydia leaning against the counter, her face in her hands. At the creak of the door, she raised her head. When Jonah saw her tear-ravaged face, he forgot his plan to take it slow. In four strides, he was across the kitchen.

"What happened? Are you all right?" It was a foolish question. She looked far from all right. He quickly scanned the kitchen. "Where's Caleb? Is he all right?"

Sniffling, she hastily scrubbed her hands over her face and straightened from her slump. "Caleb's all right. He fell asleep." Her tone was nasally. She'd been crying for a while.

Jonah ached to draw her into his arms. To pull her to his chest, rub her back and tell her it was going to be all right. But he didn't know what "it" was. "It" may not be all right at all.

"Your *daed*?" But he knew Henry was gone, having earlier helped the man load a section of a plow that needed repaired into the cart trailing Henry's buggy to take it to the blacksmith.

Lydia shook her head. More tears seeped out at the mention of her father. Her hands fisted at her sides. "*Nee*. It's not *Daed*. But I should tell him."

Asking questions obviously wasn't getting him anywhere. Surrendering to his instincts, Jonah pulled her into his embrace. She braced her forearms against his chest for a moment before rigidness drained from her limbs and, snuffling, she pressed her face against his shirt. Her shoulders shook with her continued weeping.

Jonah might not've known what to do when Rebecca cried. But with Lydia, he wanted to bear the brunt of every shuddering breath she took against his chest and absorb every tear that wet his shoulder.

"Tell him what?" he whispered as he rested his cheek against her hair, uncaring of the hairpin securing her *kapp* that poked him.

"Tell him that…" she drew in another hiccupping breath, "…that Lucetta is leaving."

Jonah raised his head. "Leaving?" On edge this morning in his anticipation to set his plan with Lydia in motion, he'd been sensitive to any sound and had heard a buggy come up the lane. Glancing out the window, he'd seen Lucetta and the girls arrive. With a mental shrug, he'd gone back to mudding drywall.

This probably wasn't the time to tell Lydia he didn't think much of her sister.

When Lydia would've pulled out of his arms, he tightened them about her. After a moment, she sagged against him again. "*Ja.* I don't know when, but she says she's leaving Peter and the girls to go with an *Englisch* man she's met."

Jonah inhaled sharply. This was leaving indeed. He opened his mouth to speak, but shut it to hear what Lydia was mumbling into his shirt.

"I'm trying so hard not to tell private things about people. I'm trying so hard to right my wrong. But it will never be right."

This time it was Jonah who drew Lydia back to peer into her face. "What are you talking about?" His voice was as gentle as his hands that capped her shoulders.

Lydia blotted her cheeks with her apron. She looked into Jonah's solemn face, his sincere eyes. Her lips, swollen from her crying, trembled. It was time she told. It was time she told someone. Wasn't it? Her shoulders rose before falling in a gusty exhale.

"My cousin Clara in Pennsylvania was a... rather plain girl. And shy. Very shy. I don't know why. Maybe, as her *mamm* became a widow at a young age and never remarried, they were each other's company and never needed much more than that. Though they attended church and some other community functions, they kept pretty much to themselves. Maybe they were enough for each other."

Her throat bobbed in a swallow. "I destroyed that." She didn't know if Jonah could hear her whisper. Tears burned at the backs of her eyes. She blinked against them. *How can I have any left?*

"Mary is my *daed*'s second cousin. I think the reason she invited me to stay with them was because she was thinking that another girl Clara's age in the house might've been *gut* for her. Might've helped her be less shy. Might've been a companion who would encourage her to go out and meet more *youngies* and perhaps help her find her special someone." A tear leaked out the corner of her eye to run down the side of her neck.

"Clara wasn't sure about me at first. But then she seemed excited to have someone her age around." Lydia's lips twisted bitterly. "I can be amusing when I apply myself. She started to trust me. That was her first mistake. She started to tell me things." Lydia closed her eyes. "That was her second."

She dashed a hand across her cheek against the growing flow of tears. "I had *gut* intentions when I went out East. I was going to leave my past behind. Start fresh. I wasn't sure if I was with child." She winced. "My *mamm* certainly didn't talk to us girls about anything like that. And neither did Lucetta when she was carrying Malinda. But I knew something was up and I suspected what it was. So my fresh start wasn't going to be so fresh and my past refused to be left behind." Opening her eyes, she met Jonah's somber gaze. It, and his grip that'd slid from her shoulders to cup her elbows, held her upright.

"And though it was a new place, I guess envy isn't confined to locations. I saw what a close, supportive relationship Clara enjoyed with her *mamm*. Something I would've loved to have had. Something I never would." She swallowed against the rawness in her throat. "Something I envied. Mary treated me kindly. More kindly than I deserved. Especially…" Squeezing her eyes shut for a moment, she rasped in a few breaths. "After."

"I'd met *youngies* at their church. I was new. I was…shiny. I was behaving for the most part. Both young women and men made particular efforts to ensure I knew I was invited to frolics and outings. I refused to go unless Clara was invited as well." Though her lips curved in a mocking smile, tears were dripping off her chin. "Wasn't that sweet of me? So Clara told me things she hadn't told anyone. Which girls she'd wished she could be friends with. Who she liked of the boys she'd seen, but hadn't really talked with at church. Who she'd dreamed of kissing. Who she'd longed to marry. Things that a shy girl with no friends her own age hadn't spoken of to anyone."

Jonah's jaw flexed. He could obviously tell where this was going. Lydia nodded miserably.

"It was getting more and more difficult to hide my...condition, which I had, up to this time. From everyone. But people were going to look at me. I needed them to focus on someone else. I started spreading rumors about her." She stared dully at the hollow of Jonah's throat above the open collar of his shirt. "We were at a Sunday night singing. Clara had confided she was hoping a certain boy would ask to take her home. She'd never had one do that before. I'd already gotten to know the boy. I'm *always* going to get to know a fellow who some other girl is interested in. He was a *gut* man. She had chosen wisely. I think, given time, he actually would've returned Clara's interest. But I made sure he was interested in me. As she was shy, she foolishly thought I was her friend, and, uncomfortable with some of the looks she'd been given, she stayed by my side all evening. To ask to drive me home, he had to do so in front of her.

"Clara held herself together well when he did. Because she liked me." Lydia's breath hiccupped. It was a moment before she could speak. When she did, her voice trembled. "She was even *happy* for me, though I'm sure she was horribly disappointed. But that wasn't enough for me. No, I made sure I told him, laughing, that wasn't it so funny that he'd asked me, when Clara had been mooning over him for some time. I told him other things she'd shared. He turned red. Clara went white. We were on the porch. She ran down the steps and into the darkness. It was a dark night, lots of cloud cover, threatening rain. Not terribly cold, but dark. I remember not being able to see her, but hearing her footsteps crunching on the gravel as she ran down the lane.

"I wasn't too worried. We were only two miles from her house. I knew she could walk that far if need be. Obviously I couldn't ride home with the young man now, as I had to take Cousin Mary's buggy. I figured I'd catch up with her before she'd gotten very far. I wasn't broken hearted. I wasn't really interested in him. He was a *gut* man and…" she swallowed again, "…I damage anything that's *gut*."

"As I was driving down the road, a car came up on me fast. I don't think it recognized at first what the orange slow-moving vehicle triangle on the back of the buggy meant. It whipped around me. I could hear it gaining speed again. I saw the white lights get smaller in the distance, then all of a sudden there was a sharp squeal and the lights in back went red. They stayed red for a moment, then they turned white again and I could hear the engine speed up once more. And then they went over a hill and all I could see was the reflection of their headlights on the low cloud cover."

She started to tremble. "I wouldn't have even found her if the horse hadn't shied. I didn't know why he spooked until I looked over to the side of the road and saw her lying there. She'd been wearing a black cloak. It was one of her few new garments and she'd been excited to wear it. First I thought she might be faking an injury because she was mad at me. That would be something I would've done. But Clara wasn't like that. I jumped down from the buggy, figuring then that maybe she *was* hurt." Lydia crossed her arms over her midsection. "She wasn't hurt. Her head was at a funny angle. Her eyes were open. But she wasn't hurt." Shaking in earnest now, Lydia didn't resist when Jonah wrapped his arms around her and pulled her to his chest. She sank into the warmth of his embrace, a connection, a comfort, she'd never experienced except with him. For sure and certain, she'd had more than her share of embraces, but they hadn't been for comfort. They'd been for a passion she'd never reciprocated, and had always ended, sometimes gracefully, sometimes not. Except with him.

Opening her mouth against his soft cotton shirt, she started keening. Not just crying. But keening, as if all the unhappiness, fear, shame and regret bottled inside had somehow broken the seal and were escaping. Needed to escape. Holding her tight, Jonah rocked her. It was some time before she could speak again. Her head and her eyes ached from crying. Her throat was raw. She slumped against him, exhausted. When she spoke, it was into his damp shirt.

"Other *youngies* leaving the singing came upon us. Some of them had cell phones. They called the police and others from the district.

They knew what to do. They came and took her. I didn't know how to face her *mamm*. It was my fault."

Weary beyond measure, she sucked in a breath, and held it before letting it out with a hiss. "Her *mamm* was forgiving. Even though I'm sure her heart ached, Mary said it was *Gott's* will. She forgave the kids that were driving the car."

"And you?" She felt the question, rather than heard it, as it vibrated from his chest.

Lydia weakly rolled her head back and forth. "She said I'd done nothing that needed to be forgiven." Apparently she was capable of another sob after all, as one wracked her. "I was too cowardly and ashamed to tell her it was all my fault.

"After Clara died, I couldn't stand myself. I was responsible for her death. I wanted to be someone else." A weak ironic laugh shuddered from her. "I've always wanted to be someone else. Someone worthy. Someone likable. I tried to make myself likable by being the one who 'knew things,' whether they were true or not. Knew negative things about people who actually were likable, so people would like me over them. Or if they didn't like me, that way it was because of my behavior, and not who I really was. I mean, if my mother couldn't think of anything to like about me, why would anyone else? If girls wouldn't like me, at least boys seemed to. And sometimes I made myself believe that just for a few moments, that they really did. But it never lasted more than those few moments. And every time I did something like that, I liked myself even less."

Lydia curled her fingers into her palms to keep from wrapping her arms about him. *Except with you, you always made me feel different. Like it really was real. Or maybe it was because I wanted so badly for it to be with you.*

With a sigh, she wedged her elbows between them and leaned back. With great hesitation, he loosened his arms from about her. The loss of his embrace was like stepping from in front of a warm fire immediately into a Wisconsin blizzard. Raising an arm, she wiped her remaining tears on her sleeve.

"How can I tell someone's secrets when I've vowed to be better. Wouldn't it be betraying a confidence? What do I do now?"

Lydia didn't resist when, with a gentle hand on her shoulder, Jonah guided her to the table and into a seat. Taking one himself, he reached out to cover her hand with his.

"I was a young teenager when my sister

Gail left. One day she was there, the next day she was gone. My sister Hannah knew she was going. I think she tried to stop her. But Gail thought she had reasons that it would be better if she left. My folks were devastated. I've never seen them…like that." Mouth grim, Jonah shook his head. "I don't know what they would've done if they'd known beforehand. But at least they would've known she was leaving. Maybe found out why she thought she needed to go. Had a chance to see if they could've changed her mind. Instead, for years, they, and I, wondered why she'd left. I think, at least in their case, it was worse not knowing."

His hand gently tightened over hers. "It's up to you. I can understand why you feel it would be a betrayal to Lucetta if you told your father. But I can understand why he'd want to know. He might try to stop her. She might be angry." He nodded his head toward the direction of the bedrooms. "But think about how you'd feel if it was Caleb planning on leaving."

Lydia stiffened. Her breath hitched. She couldn't imagine Caleb disappearing. Not knowing where he was going or why. Not being able to say goodbye. Her legs tightened as if to rise from the chair and check on him before she resettled on her seat. Jonah was right. This was different. Besides, there were the little girls involved. She needed to tell. Lydia gave him a trembling smile with lips so blubbery from crying, they didn't feel part of her face.

"I must look a mess." A flush was rising up her neck, but as red as she was from crying, he surely couldn't tell. She eased her hand out from under his.

With his fingertips, he pulled his damp shirt away from his chest. "I wouldn't be surprised if your well isn't a bit dry by now. Can I get you a drink?"

Lydia lurched to her feet. "Oh dear. You came in for dinner." She looked about the kitchen as if something to eat might suddenly appear.

He lightly caught her wrist. "That's all right—I'm the sandwich guy, remember? Do you have bread? Church spread?"

Slipping free, she hastened about the kitchen, soon sliding a plate in front of him with thick slices of homemade bread with a generous slab of peanut butter and marshmallow crème mixture between them, along with some pickled beets, cookies and a glass of milk. At his insistence, she made a smaller sandwich for herself before sitting down again at the table.

Lydia stared at the contents of the plate in front of her. She felt hollow. A hollowness that was nothing a church spread sandwich, any number of them, would ever fill.

Chapter Sixteen

In the end, it didn't matter. Lucetta had already left. She was gone before Lydia could tell her father when he arrived home later that afternoon. Lucetta had dropped the girls off with an elderly neighbor with no word of her plans. The neighbor, when no one picked the little ones up, brought them home that evening to find a bewildered Peter.

Lucetta hadn't taken anything with her. Why would she? It was a life she'd wanted to leave behind. But those she'd left behind were reeling. Jonah checked in with Lydia before he went home to help with milking. Self-conscious over her earlier loss of control, she assured him she was fine. From the kitchen window, her gaze followed him to the barn where he collected his horse and hitched it to his buggy.

Now he knows how awful I am. Now he knows, between me and my sister, how much better off he is having no connection to our family. Why would anyone want to? Lydia turned away from the window. She wasn't fine at all.

After having gone to Lucetta's home to confirm her absence, Henry was quiet that evening. Unusually so. The table was silent except for the occasional *clink* of silverware against a plate and Caleb's sporadic gibberish. Even Jacob, though hardly loquacious, barely spoke a word during supper and found an excuse to leave as soon as it was over. When Lydia finished cleaning up the kitchen, she took Caleb into the common room to play a while before bed. Every time she glanced over at her father, he was frowning as he stared at *The Budget*, the Amish newspaper, without turning a page.

As she wasn't sleeping anyway, she was out of bed early the next morning. Even so, she'd barely made her way into the kitchen when a buggy pulled into the lane. Jonah? Lydia frowned at the clock. It was early, even for him. Her hands stilled in the process of making *kaffi* when her brother-in-law Peter descended from the rig, looking decades older than she knew him to be. Reaching the ground, he stood, slump-shouldered for a moment, before leaning back into the buggy. When he turned around, he had a little girl in each arm.

Lydia met them at the bottom of the porch steps. Fannie slid into her arms without protest. Malinda had a little hand hooked around her father's neck. Peter followed Lydia into the kitchen. The arriving trio settled around the table. Lydia hastily filled plates with bread and jam and set them on the table, along with glasses of milk for the girls and a large cup of *kaffi* in front of their father.

Pale, with large shadows under his eyes, Peter probably mirrored her appearance.

"None of us slept," he responded listlessly to her questioning glance. Stirring two teaspoons of sugar into his coffee, his gaze rested on the girls, who with wary eyes and tentative fingers were eating their bread while he left his own untouched. Gripping the cup with both hands as if to warm them, Peter leaned back and closed his eyes. When he opened them again, Lydia wanted to weep anew at the look in them.

"I've thought about it all night." He sighed heavily. "They are such *gut* girls, but I can't keep them with me. Not all the time. Not and be able to do enough work to keep the farm going. And if I don't keep the farm going, I won't have a place for us to live anyway."

Above his short beard, his lips pressed into a thin line. "I've got no other local relatives in the area. I know the community will help all they can. But right now, I'm too..." his chin dropped until he was speaking into his coffee cup. "I know it's being proud, but right now I'm too humiliated to ask for or accept it." Peter shook his head. "Maybe later."

He stared numbly into the steaming black liquid. "I don't have the funds to hire anyone for their care." He snorted derisively. "And it's not like I can find a new wife to do so."

"I'd be happy to take the girls in for however long you need." Lydia didn't want to make him ask. What she saw in his gaze, when he lifted it to her, was more than thanks enough. Having met it, Lydia raised her own to meet her *daed*'s as he entered the kitchen.

"Is that all right with you?"

Giving her an abrupt nod, he patted the backs of both little girls before resting a hand on Peter's slumped shoulder. He gave it a squeeze before moving on to sit at his place at the table, where Lydia quickly set a cup of coffee.

No, left in Lucetta's wake, none of them were fine.

* * *

Jonah pulled up beside the strange buggy in the Troyer's yard. Peter's leaden descent down the porch steps this time of day, followed by his older daughter, told him all he needed to know. Lydia stood just outside the door, hugging herself as she watched the little one trail at her father's heels as he trudged across the yard. After untying his horse, Peter leaned down to swing the girl up into his arms and hug her.

Peter was a good man. Meeting the pair at the buggy's steps, Jonah couldn't imagine facing this father's limbo of a future—with a wife, but no wife. In their faith, divorces were not allowed. To do so almost guaranteed excommunication. It was difficult to face the pain in the eyes of a man who was obviously giving up his children, even if temporarily. When Peter set the little girl down, she clung to his pant leg. A spasm crossed her father's face.

At the sight, Jonah had to swallow before he could speak. "Lydia will take *gut* care of them. We all will." Though Peter gave a small smile, it was accompanied by a clenched jaw.

Jonah squatted next to the little girl. "You look like someone who likes horses. Do you?" She regarded him warily before giving a small nod.

"I thought so. I can tell. Horse people have a special eye for the animals. What can you tell me about your *daed*'s horse?" Jonah tipped his head in the direction of the patiently waiting bay mare.

"She's nice." He leaned closer in order to hear the quiet words.

"Does she have a name?"

The girl nodded again. "Pepper."

"Oh, that's a *wunderbar* name. Is she fast?"

Another nod, more decisive this time.

"Do you think she's as fast as my gelding?" Jonah gestured in the direction of his horse.

The girl released her grasp of her father's pants to turn in the direction of the sleek brown gelding. Tilting her head, she considered the animal that towered over her, before nodding her head.

Jonah smiled. "Ajax will be disappointed you think so, because he used to run on a racetrack. But loyalty is a *gut* thing. How about I pick you up, we'll say goodbye to your *daed* and then we go meet Ajax. He might try to change your mind that Pepper is faster than he is. Then we'll put him up in the barn where he can rest while I go to work."

Another hesitation, followed by a nod. Upon carefully picking her up, he met Peter's grateful gaze. "You'll see your *daed* in a while. In fact, I wouldn't be surprised if he comes over for supper sometime. Maybe he should. Your aunt Lydia is a *gut* cook. In the meantime, I'll show you what I've been working on." Shifting her in his arms, Jonah pointed to the addition. "See that big section of the house? It's empty. Can you believe that? There's nothing in it. No beds. No chairs. All empty, because I'm still building it. Would you like to see it after we take care of Ajax? *Ja?* Well, we'll let your *daed* get on his way, then we'll get started. Sounds like we already have a bit of a busy day. And you know what? If Aunt Lydia doesn't keep you busy, maybe you could help me out. I'm mudding drywall. Would you like to help me put goop on the wall in the places I tell you to?"

He was rewarded with a timid smile. Taking a step away from Peter, he gave the man a robust wave, which the little girl echoed. As the other man stepped up into his buggy, Jonah held the little girl up to meet the brown gelding, who nuzzled her arm, eliciting a tiny giggle. When Peter's buggy headed down the lane, Jonah unhitched his horse and, setting the girl on the gelding's back, led him to the barn. When they made the return trip across the barnyard a short while later after taking care of the animal, he walked side by side with one he now knew as Malinda, her miniature hand clasped in his calloused one.

Lydia, hands twisting together, had been watching out the window for their return. When they entered the kitchen through the mudroom door, she was helping Fannie down from her chair at the table.

Jonah met her anxious gaze. "I've got a new helper here. We'll be working in the addition if you need us."

"If you're sure?" Her gaze darted between the pair. Both were wearing smiles.

He nodded. "It'll be all right, Lydia. By the way, I invited Peter for supper sometime. I know it wasn't my place, but the situation seemed to call for it."

"Of course. *Denki.* I wish I'd thought of it." Lydia watched the two disappear into the addition, Malinda skipping along beside her much taller escort. Closing the door, she looked over to where Caleb was contentedly smearing his breakfast either over his face or the tray in between the bites that made it into his mouth.

What was she doing keeping this man from his child? What was she doing keeping her child from his father? Turning back toward the door, she grabbed the handle. As she twisted her wrist to open it, to call to Jonah, she recalled Peter's devastated face that morning.

Swallowing, she let go of the handle. What she was doing was saving Jonah from the same fate. Better to spare him in the long run than provide whatever brief joy would be in the short one.

Lydia slipped the warm eggs into her basket, grateful the hen hadn't minded being disturbed from the nest. Not all were so placid. But lately, any form of peace was appreciated, even the gentle clucking of the contented hens. Not that things were bad. In the past two days, the girls had adjusted very well. Surprisingly, Fannie had been content to nap when Caleb did, as they were doing now; she was probably catching up on rest from previous tension in her home. And Malinda, *ach*, she was Jonah's little shadow. When he was doing tasks where it might be dangerous to have the little one around, Malinda joined Lydia on whatever she was doing. But if Jonah could find a way to safely accommodate the girl, she was always with him.

Which meant Lydia was seeing him more, as he stopped in to pick up Malinda when he arrived, was always there for dinner and stopped again to escort the little one in before he left. Although the girl would've probably loved to go home with him.

Lydia would've too. She would've loved to *make* a home with him. Glancing at the nesting chickens, she sighed. However, rather than be with her, for Jonah's sake, it would be better for him to take up residence in a henhouse rather than live separately in a *daadi haus* like Peter had before Lucetta left, or stay out of the house as much as possible as her *daed* had while her *mamm* was alive.

Ducking out the low-hung door, Lydia squinted as she stepped into the sunlight. *Please,* Gott, *let Jonah finish the addition soon so he doesn't continue to be a daily fixture.* She didn't know how much longer she could keep from showing how much she cared for him.

Lydia jerked to a halt at the sight of a strange buggy at the hitch post. Two women diverted from their path to the porch to intercept her at the henhouse. Lydia frowned, trying to recognize the unexpected visitors. When they came closer and she did, she stiffened.

Susie looked as tense as Lydia felt, and even the widow Edna's smile appeared a little strained.

"My father isn't here." Lydia glanced toward the buggy to see if anyone else was alighting. Already, she felt considerably outnumbered. When no one appeared, she took her first full breath since she'd seen the buggy.

The widow was wringing her hands. "I know. He mentioned he'd be gone this morning on an errand."

Lydia's gaze shifted between the two. *Then why are you here?*

The older woman tipped her head toward her daughter. "Susie has something she wants to say to you."

From the looks of the young woman, she didn't want to say it too badly. But her gaze held Lydia's as she cleared her throat. "I'm sorry. I was the one who started the rumor that the little boy was yours. I overheard your father tell my *mamm*, and I... I wanted a reason not to like you."

Lydia tightened her grip on the handle of the egg basket to ensure she didn't drop it. So this was how it had gotten out so fast. "Uh...um..." Not knowing what else to do, she dipped her chin in a brief nod.

"I hope you'll forgive her." The widow's brows were furrowed over troubled eyes.

Lydia's gaze darted back to the younger

woman's face. "There's nothing to forgive. It was true."

"Be that as it may. But it shouldn't have been shared, and particularly not with a malicious intent. I raised her better than that."

Lydia gave a weak smile before hunching her shoulders, waiting for the tirade to burst from mother to daughter as the girl was disciplined.

"*Denki*, Susie." The widow put her hand on her daughter's forearm. Her voice was quiet. "I'm not pleased with what you did, but I am proud of you for taking responsibility for it and apologizing."

Nodding, Susie exhaled and hung her head.

The widow's smile, though small, looked sincere. "I don't suppose we'll need to have this discussion again?"

Shuffling her feet, the younger woman shook her head. For a lingering moment, the only sounds were those of the farmyard—the chickens in the henhouse, a horse neighing in the barn. Raising her head, Susie met Lydia's gaze with a hesitant smile before glancing away. She cleared her throat. "You have a well-maintained farm. May I…look around?"

"Certainly." Lydia gestured with an open hand for the girl to help herself. Susie drifted off, leaving Lydia with the widow.

"We are terribly sorry. Henry was a bit… distressed and so he told me of your news. Susie…" her gaze followed her daughter as the young woman headed for the big white barn. "She was close to her *daed*. She's having a hard time adjusting to the change with him gone." The woman grimaced. "Well, we all were. We were hoping my husband would recover. But we have to trust *Gott* even though things aren't as we might hope. As it says in Proverbs, 'Trust in the Lord with all thine heart; and lean not unto thine own understanding. In all thy ways acknowledge Him, and He shall direct thy paths.'

"I believe He's directing my path to Henry. Your father makes me happy. I hope to make him happy. I know you don't have any reason to trust us after this. I hope you'll give Susie a chance." Her gaze rested on where her daughter lingered at a fence, trying to coax the draft horses inside over to her.

"She really is a good girl. Just a little unsettled right now. She doesn't like the thought of moving out of the house she was raised in. I'm thinking Mary Ann and the neighbor boy will have an announcement made in church soon, so Susie, my youngest, would be moving, to her mind, by herself, should your father and I marry.

"Although Susie hasn't warmed up to him yet, your father is a *gut* man. One I'd be glad to join with." The creases at the corners of the woman's eyes wrinkled as her smile expanded. "I'd truly be glad to join with you and your son as well."

"She likes barns and livestock?" Lydia watched as Susie entered the barn through the Dutch door.

"Oh *ja*. I could never keep her in the house—she was always out working with her *daed*." The woman gave a contented shrug. "But as long as they were happy, so was I."

Lydia inhaled deeply as she studied the widow—though she had to quit thinking of her that way. She was Edna. "What are your feelings about having two little girls in the house when you marry my father?"

Chapter Seventeen

That evening, Lydia told her *daed* about the unexpected visit.

"I know what I think in this doesn't matter. But I do think you made a *gut* choice with Edna."

And she did. Maybe she was being fooled as well; time would tell. What the widow— Lydia corrected herself, Edna—had said about trusting *Gott* had struck her. She believed in *Gott*, but did she *really* trust Him?

Her *daed* hadn't responded beyond meeting her gaze, but a hint of a smile had lifted the corner of his lips. And he wore the biggest grin she'd seen on his face, particularly in the past few weeks, when he came home late in the evening that Visiting Sunday. It seemed like Edna and Susie would be moving in soon.

Lydia waited for the lurch in her stomach at the realization. It didn't occur. She was dwelling instead on the visitors she'd had that day. She'd been playing with Caleb on a blanket she'd laid under a big oak tree in the yard when a buggy clattered up the lane and Grace Kauffman, Miriam, Rebecca and Rachel—along with her twins—had bounded out.

Lydia was still in awe of the afternoon. They'd talked, laughed, had *kaffi* and shared cookies that the arrivals had brought along. Rachel was naturally a quieter person, and Rebecca had seemed surprisingly so, but Miriam had made sure there were no lapses in the conversation. Though the way the young wife had looked at Caleb and, with a smile, touched her midsection, indicated there was something the blonde woman hadn't told.

Was this what it was like to have friends? Who accepted her as…herself? If they hadn't seen personally, they'd surely heard what she was. A few had experienced some of the worst of it. And they'd still come to visit? To include her? Yet by this time next week, these women, all church members—one in particular who had reason to judge her harshly—would be voting on whether or not to shun her.

How would she treat them if the situation

was reversed? How would she treat a woman with a venomous tongue and actions who was getting her comeuppance? Would she visit, laugh, share cookies and admire an illegitimate son? Lydia didn't know what to think.

Her head might've been in turmoil, but her heart knew what it wanted when Jonah poked his head in the kitchen door Monday morning. He smiled at the sight of the children contentedly playing on the floor while she was rolling out pie dough.

"You're *gut* at this."

"I...am I?" If all the warm joy that flooded her could be directed, she wouldn't need to turn on the oven to bake the pie.

"Just ask them."

Swiveling from the counter, Lydia regarded the trio. She rolled her eyes. "Two of them can't really talk."

"Not by words maybe, but in other ways, they certainly can. Not all communication is verbal." His smile expanded to a grin. "You'd know if you worked with cows more."

Inhaling sharply at the amused glint in his green eyes and the dark curls that seemed already almost threatening to obscure them, Lydia decided being mute was the better course of action. She turned back around to face the dough that now wedged high on one side and tapered to nothing on the other.

"I've got something that I hope will help entertain them." He'd ducked back out the door before she could respond.

Leaning to glance out the window, her jaw dropped as she watched him pull a wooden rocking horse from his buggy. When he returned to the kitchen, she hurried to hold the door open. The little girls, eyes wide as saucers, gathered around as soon as he set the horse on the floor where it rocked gently from end to end.

"Your *bruder* Jacob cut the head, tail and rounded rocking boards for me. Working at Schrock Brothers Furniture, he has access to some tools that I don't yet have. For the rest," Jonah shrugged, "I'm around plenty of leftover lumber all the time." Lumber, Lydia noted, that'd been sanded until it was smooth as glass and dyed a warm brown.

"For us?" Malinda stroked her hand over the seat.

"You're the horse girl. Until you get a little bit bigger, you need one more your size." With an eager nod, Malinda climbed onto the seat and began to rock. Lydia had to blink against the tears that threatened at the wide smile creasing the little one's face.

Fannie patiently awaited her own turn. When Malinda dismounted the wooden horse, she helped her sister on the first time. After that, the girls clambered off and on by themselves. Caleb didn't want to be left out. Scrambling over on hands and knees, he joined in the new adventure.

Pinching the edges of what was surely the worst crust she'd ever made, Lydia looked over as Jonah lifted the boy onto the horse and, keeping one hand on his back, used the other to guide Caleb's miniature hands to the handles protruding from the horse's head. Jonah hadn't interacted with the boy much lately. Partly because of Lydia's intervention in keeping or directing the boy elsewhere. It was too painful to see the two together, to watch and dream of what could never be.

But mostly because the little girls had adopted Jonah in the absence of their father. Peter had stopped by a few times. It was obvious the man was using work as a barrier against his pain, keeping himself busy either to avoid thinking of his devastating situation or trying to earn enough money to make some change, either hire help or prepare the farm for sale and return to where he was originally from, where his own family could provide support.

Lydia watched as Jonah's smile faded. Tension washed through her as his jaw flexed. His expression was in sharp contrast to the grinning boy's.

"His eye. How long has it been that way?" The words were terse.

Lydia's attention darted to Caleb. Above his big smile, one eye was directed at Jonah, while the other pointed in toward the little boy's nose. She'd been seeing the disjointed look more and more lately. Her shoulders stiffened. Was he judging her child? She wanted to race over and sweep Caleb into her arms.

"I've noticed it for a little while. Infants' eyes do that occasionally. I'm sure it will go away given time."

Jonah swept his hat off and ran a hand through his hair, revealing a vein that rose on his temple. She shrank under his hooded gaze. "And if it doesn't, you could be affecting his vision for life. Don't you think you should have it checked out?"

Unable to withstand his intensity, Lydia shifted her focus to the pie pan, where divots and crescent-shaped creases from her tense fingers pocked the dough. Was he judging her capabilities as a mother? Would she fall short there? With all her concern over her child's emotional well-being, was she failing his physical one?

She cleared her throat. "I'll think about it."

"Do that."

Though she didn't turn around, she winced at the decisive click of the mudroom door. Pulling the edges of the dough away from the pie pan, Lydia squeezed it into a lumpy ball. Apparently she wasn't good at this after all.

Jonah pressed his hand on his knee to stifle its bouncing. His heart was hammering. He knew it was possible, more than possible, but this would confirm it. His strained face matched what he could see, in the relative dimness of the room, of Lydia's from where she sat in the optometrist's chair with Caleb on her lap. The boy left no question as to his opinion on having first one eye, then the other covered, in addition to the strange device pushed up to his face and light shone into his eyes by an unknown man. He only cheered up when the doctor allowed him to take the finger puppet the man had been moving back and forth in front of the child's eyes.

Much to Jonah's relief, Lydia had agreed the next day to take Caleb to the doctor. With more prompting, a few days later, she'd agreed to let him accompany her to the local optometrist the Amish in the district frequented. Jonah didn't know if she wanted him there or not. If she didn't, it was too bad. He was going.

Having brightened the soft lights, the doctor leaned against the counter and smiled reassuringly between Jonah and Lydia. "It's a good thing you brought him in. What we're dealing with is an accommodative esotropia. That's a fancy term for what is otherwise known as a..." He paused and looked over when Jonah jerked his arms up to cross over his chest.

"A strabismus," Jonah finished for him, his voice hoarse. "Sometimes called cross-eyed."

Raising his eyebrows, the doctor nodded. "Being cross-eyed is common in younger babies, but usually passes by four to six months old as their eye muscles develop and strengthen. As he's a bit older than that, it's something we need to treat to make sure it doesn't progress to amblyopia, or lazy eye, which can affect the development of clear vision."

Her face pale, Lydia wrapped her arms around the boy on her lap. "Will he lose his vision?"

"No. Caught this early there's very good success on treating it."

"Where did it come from?"

Without his hand to suppress it, Jonah's knee was visibly bouncing. The doctor's news was what he'd expected. What he hadn't anticipated was the flood of emotion at having it confirmed. But he had the answer for Lydia's question.

"My youngest brother and I had it when we were babies. As did my father. It's genetic."

Smiling, the doctor nodded again, like Jonah was a prize student in school. "That would make sense. It can run in families and some studies have shown it's particularly attributed to the father. It's a good thing you brought your son in. How is your vision now?"

Jonah's gaze was locked on Lydia. If her face was pale before, it was nothing compared to its current state. "I can see just fine now."

Lydia's slender throat bobbed in a hard swallow. Her arms briefly tightened around Caleb, *his son*, like she wanted to rise from the chair with the boy and dash out of the room. His legs flexed to follow if she did. *So the truth has come out. At least on this.*

Lydia barely heard the doctor over the buzzing in her ears. The man spoke of fitting Caleb for glasses with prisms in them, ones that would tell his eyes where they needed to focus, helping the weaker muscles strengthen and in time, correcting the strabismus. Caleb wouldn't like the glasses at first, of course, but the doctor assured her they would have a strap to secure them and that babies did get used to them after a while.

It would all have to be explained to her again. Sometime when she could pay attention. While she heard the words the man spoke, they made no sense. The only thing that kept throbbing through her head was that he *knew*. Jonah *knew* that Caleb was his son. Though she dropped her gaze, the weight of his pinned her into the seat. Even if she denied Caleb's parentage again, Jonah wouldn't believe it.

"If you have any questions, let me know. There are some handouts in the outer office. I've got what information I need for the lenses and we have some standard frames for the little ones, if that's all right with you."

Lydia gave the doctor a quavering smile and a nod. Her thank-you was barely above a whisper. She was surprised she had the breath for that; her chest was so tight. Jonah was silent as he followed her from the room and back to the counter in the main office. When she noticed him paying the bill she couldn't afford while the attendant showed her the glasses and went back over instructions, heat crept up her neck and over her cheeks. The attendant, thinking it was because of the instructions, hastened to assure her.

"It's not as complicated as it might seem. You'll do fine. As will he."

One glance at Jonah's face and it was obvious "fine" wasn't going to be an option. With another breathless thank-you, she ducked out of the office and headed for the buggy with Jonah following behind at a measured pace. Nervous, worried, wanting some support for what might be determined regarding Caleb's eyes, she'd invited Jonah along. She never imagined the diagnosis would create greater anxiety, but for a different reason. Dread pooled in her stomach at the upcoming ride home.

When she slid open the buggy's door, Jonah reached out to take the boy, allowing her to climb in unencumbered. It was how they'd entered the buggy to drive in this morning. Then, the action had drawn her pensive smile. But now, *now* Jonah knew he would be holding his own son. When she hesitated, he just waited. Caleb didn't help when he leaned toward Jonah with outstretched arms. Shifting the boy to her opposite hip, she awkwardly scrambled into the buggy.

"Why did you lie to me?"

Keeping her gaze on the buggy's wooden dash, Lydia fisted her apron in damp palms. "I wasn't sure who Caleb's father might be— there were so many possibilities."

"You're lying to me again. There wasn't anyone else, was there? Or if there was, it was a lot fewer than it appeared."

"I…"

"Men talk too, Lydia. And it was with great relief a lot of the district's young men admitted that what they'd implied about being with you had never happened. Did it?"

Lifting her gaze, she stared ahead at the twitching ears of the horse. Caleb tugged one of her *kapp* ribbons into his mouth. A car pulled into the parking lot, the arrival looking at them as the woman made her way into the optometrist's office. After untying his horse, Jonah agilely climbed in beside Lydia. The bench seat, and the distance between them, hadn't felt this small on the drive in.

"At least not with them."

Lydia winced. He wasn't going to let it go. Of course he wasn't going to. The man just found out he had a son.

"So why me?"

I can't change the fact that he knows, but I can still drive him away. It took a few deep breaths before she was able to do so, and concentration, but Lydia was able to frame a smirk on her face. She glanced over, letting her gaze run up and down him. "Why not you? You're handsome. You have prospects." With a stab to her own heart, she twisted the ugly smile further. "You were a challenge."

Jonah shook his head as he gathered up the lines and backed the horse away from the hitch. "*Nee.* You're lying again. You do that when you're afraid, don't you?"

"I'm not afraid of you," she countered.

"I'm glad to hear it. You shouldn't be." He studied her face. "*Nee*, it's not me you're afraid of. It's us. Of being with someone who honestly cares for you."

Flushing, Lydia scooted closer to the buggy's door. Jonah reached out and captured her wrist in a gentle grip. "Give us a try, Lydia. Marry me."

Her heart lurched. She was too stunned to even attempt to jerk her hand free. It was all she'd ever wanted. All she could never have. Tears burned behind her eyes and in the back of her throat, making her voice hoarse. "No. I can't marry you. I won't marry you."

"Why not?" His tone matched the gaze that bored into her.

Lydia bit the inside of her cheek. It was so

hard to meet the eyes that matched her son's, apparently matched in more ways than she could've imagined. "I don't love you."

"You're lying again."

She tugged her hand free. "I don't want to love you. I don't want you to be his father." Jonah looked like she'd slapped him as the words tumbled from her mouth. Though the Amish rejected violence, Lydia might've felt better if she had. She knew words could hurt as bad or worse. She started to tremble.

There was nothing she wanted more than to be a family with Jonah, Caleb and whatever additional children *Gott* might give to them. But that was selfish. It might be best for her. Stifling a whimper, her face crumpled as she tightened her arms about her son. It would be best for Caleb. But for Jonah, it would be a tragedy to be tied to her.

Jonah's voice was as rigid as his profile. "I'm going to be a part of Caleb's life."

She hissed in a breath. "Give me time to figure out a way for that to happen to some extent."

"I don't want it to *some* extent. We're going to get married. We're going to be a family. I'm his father. He's my child. You have to admit it, Lydia. You've spent your life telling things that may or may not be true about others. This *is* true about us." A muscle flexed in his jaw. "If you won't tell. I will."

"Oh, Jonah. In a week's time I'll, in all likelihood, be shunned. Is that what you want for a wife? Look at Peter. Haven't you learned anything from what he's facing?"

She was trapped. Her rapid breathing was making her light-headed. In an attempt to regain control of herself, she counted her breaths in and out as she had when she was a child under her mother's tirades. Caleb squirmed indignantly until she loosened her arms from about him.

Jonah was a man of convictions. Lydia squeezed her eyes shut as if to block out the knowledge. Convictions he'd forsaken for her. He wouldn't sway on this. A man should parent his child. Should marry and support the child's mother. If she stayed in the area, there would be no dissuading him.

So she wouldn't stay.

Mary would let her come back. Amazing Mary, who'd supported her return to Wisconsin because she'd known Lydia needed to confront her past here, would welcome her and Caleb back to Pennsylvania. If their presence caused her pain because they were there instead of her daughter, she'd never let it show. Maybe she'd even appreciate the company.

But how could she go, when, for the first time in her life, she was beginning to like herself here? When she was realizing she could have friends not because they were afraid to be on her bad side, but who refused to *see* her bad side? Women she admired, who drew her into their circle, unworthy though she was?

And Jonah. Who was so good with her son. With his son.

Jonah, who should have many more sons and daughters with a wife who would be a blessing to him instead of a curse.

Lydia cleared her throat, one restricted with regret. "Some folks already believe that I couldn't identify Caleb's father even if I wanted to. If you tell anyone that it's you, of all people, they won't believe you. They'll think I tricked you into claiming him." Lydia shuddered in a few breaths before she could continue. "If you tell that you're his father, Caleb and I will go back to Pennsylvania. So, do you want to be able to occasionally see him, or do you want him permanently out of your life?"

Chapter Eighteen

Jonah stared unseeing as he poured milk through the strainer into the stainless steel milk cans. Setting the pail down, he then numbly screwed on the can's lid before lifting the heavy container into the big tank where it joined several others. The tank, filled with chilly water currently lapping at the milk cans' handles, served a dual purpose. Once it'd cooled the milk, the now warmer water would be released to run into the stock tank and water the cows. Though warmer water wasn't a factor in the fall, when winter and freezing temperatures hit, the setup was very beneficial indeed.

The idea hadn't been his, but his father's from some time back. Jonah scowled. *Gut* thing someone was thinking. He didn't know if he was capable of it anymore. The only thing running through his mind since he'd left the optometrist's earlier in the afternoon was that Lydia didn't want him. Didn't even want to love him. Wouldn't marry him. Didn't want him to be the father of her child. Was only going to let him have peripheral access to his son—*his son*—if at all. And if he told, as his heart was bursting to do, they'd both be gone.

He was a father, but he wasn't. Jonah rubbed a hand across the ache in his chest. Kind of like Peter. His hand stilled. Peter, whose situation was tragic. Lydia had mentioned learning from Peter. What had she meant?

"Are you all right?"

Jonah looked over to where his father was entering from the milking parlor, a stainless steel bucket in each hand. All right? He hadn't been all right since he'd noticed Caleb's eye days earlier and became all but certain the boy was his son. And that Lydia had blatantly lied about it. *"Nee."* He grimaced. "Not really."

"I wondered, when you showed up at home in the middle of the afternoon." Zebulun began pouring milk into the clean can Jonah had automatically placed the strainer over. He raised an eyebrow at his son. "You decide you'd rather be a dairyman instead of a carpenter?"

Jonah had made no decisions about anything. About anything at all. He'd just been numb. "I...there were reasons I didn't feel like working there today."

After finishing with one bucket, Zebulun tipped the other one up. "Reasons that will keep you from going back?"

"I have to go back. I have an obligation... I have obligations to fulfill. You taught me to always fulfill them. I never want to disappoint you." Dipping his chin, Jonah rubbed his chest again. The small part of his heart that wasn't bursting with joy at being Caleb's father was aching at the aspect of displeasing his folks, of forsaking the vows to his church.

Tipping the twenty-quart bucket completely upside down by its tilting handle, Zebulun watched as the final white rivulets ran from the stainless steel pail into the milk can. "You'd never disappoint me. I trust and pray for *Gott* to lead your path, and if," Zebulun slanted a glance at Jonah, "and when, you step away from it, that He will lead you back."

Setting the lid on the can, Jonah began to tighten it. "I just don't want to cause you grief."

"*Ach.* Not want to cause me grief? And you still keep pestering me with all these ideas you have?" The admonishment was softened by the small smile Zebulun sent in his direction. "I love you, son. That won't change. No matter what you do. Even if you decide to work with wood instead of cows. But as long as you're working with cows..." his father tipped his head toward the door, from which the sounds of contented bovine and the bantering of Jonah's brothers filtered through. "These buckets aren't going to carry themselves in from the parlor. Are you ready?"

Giving the lid a final twist, Jonah then hefted it into the tank with the others. He stared across the large collection of stainless steel cans. Could he ever be truly ready for the possible loss of the son he'd just discovered?

Lydia looked in the direction of Caleb's pointing finger. "*Ja.* That's a goat." The little black doe bleated as if in answer. Other does and kids in the pasture took up the chorus. Caleb clapped his hands in delight.

"Susannah has lots of goats, doesn't she?" Lydia couldn't blame the animals for their utterances. Their normally quiet farm had been taken over by children of various ages playing in the yard and women moving back and forth between the garden and the house. All had descended to pick and can late season tomatoes so the new mother would have an ample supply of canned tomatoes and juice stored in her basement.

Rachel had reminded Lydia of the event during her visit Sunday. Though Lydia had intended to attend, she'd gone out to the barn to harness her *daed*'s horse with great reluctance. In fact, she'd gone out twice, the first time returning to the house before calling herself a coward. Only her respect and admiration for Susannah, and Lydia's growing friendship with Susannah's daughters Rachel and Rebecca, had prompted her to drag her feet back outside and finish the hitching.

Even so, she'd looked longingly back toward her house as she drove down the lane, apprehensive about facing people of her district when she'd face them again in the church service tomorrow and, more dreadfully, what followed. Tomorrow was her kneeling confession, followed by a possible—*highly* possible—shunning. She couldn't stop the coming events from worrying at her mind like a puppy at a shoe.

Following the church service, after all guests and nonmembers were dismissed, the bishop would ask her to come forward and kneel by the ministers in the midst of the congregation. Lydia's cheeks heated, knowing she'd be asked several questions about her offense and if she planned to cease the offending activity. That particular response was a resounding yes. As for the questions? Lydia swallowed. She could answer all but who had been involved with her. She wouldn't divulge who Caleb's father was.

Then she would leave the gathering and the bishop would advise the congregation of the punishment determined by the ministers earlier that morning. After which a vote—*der Rat*—would occur, where each member would be asked if they agreed with the suggested punishment, which they usually did.

So Lydia was preparing herself for a unanimous vote and subsequent shunning. She'd need to set two tables for dinner, as others in her household wouldn't be allowed to eat at the same one with her. She wouldn't even be able to hand Caleb directly off to her father. Or Jonah. To transfer the boy, she'd have to set him down first and allow the other person to pick him up. Her stomach twisted. Not that Jonah would want anything to do with her now.

She brushed a hand over her son's wispy

hair. If that was their future, maybe it would be *gut* if he learned to walk soon. As if in answer, Caleb crawled off her lap and, tugging on her sleeve to steady himself, stood on the rough concrete of the cistern cap on which she sat.

Still, she'd take the upcoming humiliating confession three times over rather than re-live yesterday's visit to the eye doctor and the resulting stilted ride home afterward with Jonah. They hadn't spoken for the duration. Lydia winced at the memory. It would've been difficult for Jonah to do so, as tight as his jaw had been.

When they'd arrived home, he'd come around to help her down from the buggy. This time Caleb had leaned so far in his direction the boy would've tipped out of her arms if Jonah hadn't caught him. She'd followed them into the house, suppressing tears at the sight that, although Jonah's jaw was like granite, his hand rubbed gentle circles on the boy's back. Once in the kitchen, he'd set the child carefully on the floor, shot a final look at her, gone out to the buggy and driven away.

Lydia had tried to tell herself he was leav-ing because it was close to milking time, but there'd been a good bit of afternoon left. No, he'd left because he couldn't stand to be around her. Why would he? She'd hurt him deeply. Again. She was always hurting him. So, it was better that he learned to stay away from her. She sniffed. At the moment, it felt like nothing would ever be better again.

Maybe she should leave, as she'd threatened. That way, Jonah could get on with his life. Maybe it would be *gut* to go now. After the six-week ban, when she still didn't admit who Caleb's father was, it would be thought she'd shown no remorse and she'd be excommunicated anyway.

Her fingers pressed against the cistern cap's rough concrete surface. How could she leave the girls? They needed consistency. Security. Peter may not be ready yet to take them back. Lydia's shoulders relaxed as Edna's pleasant face came to mind. The soon-to-be not widow would care for them. Lydia smiled ruefully. If the couple married during her ban, it would certainly be awkward to sit at a table all by herself at the wedding.

More buckets of tomatoes were carried by. With a sigh, Lydia forced herself from her melancholy. She couldn't change tomorrow, and she couldn't change yesterday, but today, she needed to join in and get to work.

Clasping Caleb to her hip, she scooted off the knee-high concrete cap and stood, brushing off the back of her skirt. She strode over to where the older girls were already watching Malinda and Fannie along with other little ones, and handed Caleb over. Snorting softly, she grabbed a bucket and headed to the garden. Good thing the canning event was this week instead of next. She'd be poor help if no one could take anything directly from her hand.

An hour later, Lydia was elbow deep in a sink full of bobbing tomatoes, part of an efficient assembly line in blanching, peeling, slicing or juicing—whichever was needed—and so on in the process of canning. Surprisingly, she was enjoying herself more than she'd expected. She'd seen Susannah, admired the baby, been sincerely welcomed into the group and had peeled dozens of tomatoes. And, to her relief, for the most part, had been able to put aside thoughts of tomorrow and Jonah.

Lydia had just fished out the last tomato from the sink when Malinda ran up and tugged on her skirt. The little girl's eyes dominated her pale face. Seeing her distress, Lydia squatted to her level.

"What is it?"

"Caleb fell in a hole. He disappeared." The words came out in a rush.

Lydia was sure she hadn't heard right. Even

so, her heart began galloping. She jerked upright. "What?"

"Caleb fell in a hole. We can't see him."

Dropping the tomato into the sink with a splash, Lydia dashed through the nearest door and sprinted for the backyard. One of the older girls who'd been watching the little ones intercepted her. The girl's face was ashen. "Four of the boys pushed the cap a ways off the cistern and couldn't get it back on again. Then someone found a baseball and they left the lid as it was and started playing ball. We'd been watching closely, but two of the other little ones bumped heads and were crying and while we were attending to them, Caleb crawled over to the cistern. Before we could get there, he'd pulled himself up on the edge and toppled over into the open space between the rim and the cap. We looked in, but it's dark down there and we can't see him."

Frantic, Lydia sprinted on to where the thick round concrete cap was slid off its perch. Instead of covering the large hole once used to catch and hold rainwater for the farm's use, a dark gap of about a foot yawned at the edge. Everything below the gap was pitch-black. The rough concrete abraded her palms as Lydia threw her weight against the heavy lid. The grate of stone on stone rent the air as it slid open another inch. Why wasn't Caleb crying? He should be crying. How deep was the cistern? Was there water in the bottom? Was that why he wasn't crying?

With a groan, she lunged against the lid again. This time the heavy cap slid more easily, opening up another dark foot. Lydia glanced to the side to see Rachel and Rebecca shoving in unison with her. Their momentum had the women teetering briefly over the lip of the cistern before they caught themselves. On her hands and knees, Lydia frantically scanned the dank-smelling depths of the hole. The bottom was still in shadows. There was no sound of splashing. Was that good or bad?

"Caleb!"

At the wail that erupted from the shadows, Lydia burst into tears. She leaned forward, ready to spring into the pit, but a hand on her shoulder held her back. She looked up to see Miriam. "Hannah is getting a flashlight. Susannah went to get Jethro, who's working in the barn. He'll bring a ladder. We'll have Caleb out in no time."

Hannah, Jonah's oldest sister, fell to her knees beside Lydia, extending a heavy silver flashlight. Fumbling for a moment to flick it on, Lydia finally succeeded and swept the beam into the hole. It flashed over bricks and plaster that lined the cistern down to the bottom. Lydia's shoulders eased a fraction when the light revealed no water in the receptacle. The pit had once been deeper, but when the cistern had no longer been used, one of the previous owners had apparently begun filling it with debris—plastic bottles, old feed bags, cans—that were jumbled inside in a makeshift pyramid that reached up from the bottom.

The beam caught and held on her son's pale, upturned face. At the sight of blood, Lydia stifled a moan. Caleb strengthened his cry and tried to crawl toward the light but kept sliding down the stack of paper feed sacks he'd apparently landed on. Lydia took the movement of his limbs as a good sign. She wheezed in a breath as she recognized his cry as one not necessarily of pain, but of fear and anger.

"It's okay. I'm right here. I'll be down to you as fast as I can!"

Initially the cistern had been about fifteen feet deep; the added rubble had reduced the distance. Lydia eyed it. If she hung by her hands from the edge and then let go, she could drop that far.

Swinging her legs over the lip, she flexed her hands as she looked for the best place to grip. Caleb's wail surged when he slid down the slanted debris. Lydia hesitated. What if she landed on top of him and injured him further?

"Jethro's coming with a ladder!"

Looking over her shoulder, she saw Jethro Weaver, Susannah's husband, approaching from the barn at a trot. A long wooden ladder banged against his legs. Scrambling to her feet when Jethro set the ladder down, Lydia joined him in pushing the cap completely off its base. Retrieving the ladder, he carefully lowered it into the pit, leaning over the edge and adjusting the rails until there was a semblance of stability. The cistern depth exceeded the ladder's length. The grayed wood rails ended a few inches below the edge, knocking plaster as it grated against the bricks that rimmed the pit. Lydia could barely hear Jethro over Caleb's wailing that echoed up the cistern.

"I'm going d-down first. I want t-to check him out to m-make sure, if he's injured, that we d-don't add to it. You can follow m-me d-down to b-be on hand to reassure the little one." The man's voice was calm and steady around his natural stutter.

Though frantic to get to her son, Lydia nodded, knowing that as one of the local volunteer firemen, Jethro had training in first aid.

"Rachel and Rebecca, help secure the ladder." Jethro swung over the mouth of the pit and began his descent.

As soon as the top of his straw hat disappeared over the lip of the hole, Lydia scrambled for a secure footing on the ladder. Sliding her hands quickly down the ladder's rough rails, she ignored the splinters that gouged her palms. She wobbled a moment as she stepped off the last rung and onto the uneven debris before clambering over the pile of refuse to where Jethro was cautiously approaching a wailing Caleb. The boy's eyes were swimming in tears that streamed, along with blood, down his face. Lydia scrutinized what she could see of him. Beyond his being smeared with dust and cobwebs, a small cut high on his forehead was the only source she could see of the blood.

"Hi, fella. I just want to check you out a b-bit." Jethro ran deft hands down the boy's limbs and torso. He gently moved Caleb's fine hair to get a closer look at the cut. Screaming, Caleb reached both arms out to her. Biting her lip, Lydia crossed her arms over her chest to keep from grabbing for him. At the next sob, she could contain herself no longer and gently grasped one of his bare feet in her hand.

"I d-don't think any limbs are d-damaged. And his chest feels fine. I'd feel b-better though if we t-take him to the hospital for a closer look." Jethro carefully lifted the boy to her. "And I know he'd feel b-better to b-be in his *m-mamm*'s arms."

His *mamm* gathered him close. She certainly felt better having him there.

Caleb's sobs decreased to snuffles and whimpers. Lydia gently and cautiously rubbed his back, sensitive to any abnormalities. Tears streaking down the cheeks of mother and son, Jethro gingerly led them over the piled rubbish back to the ladder. When Lydia looked up, several concerned faces were leaning over the edge of the cistern and numerous hands were reaching out to help them. Cautiously, deftly, they assisted the trio back to the surface.

Chapter Nineteen

Had it only been a short month since she'd faced these same people lining the church benches on the day after her return to Miller's Creek? It seemed like such a long time ago, in so many ways. Lydia still felt the trepidation and shame of that morning, particularly with her upcoming confession at the end of this service. She'd come home to address her past. But, as she made eye contact with many of those present, what impacted her wasn't her behavior toward them in years past, but theirs toward her recently, when a multitude of these same faces had met her in the hospital waiting room yesterday as she'd emerged with Caleb—blessedly unscathed except for a cut too small to even require stitches and a need to cling to his mother.

Her son had been checked over numerous

times by proficient hands even before he'd arrived at the hospital. Hannah, as the district's midwife experienced in examining newborns, had assessed Caleb while they waited for her husband, Gabe, the local EMT, to arrive. Gabe had made a quick examination as well before transporting mother and child to the hospital.

This was her church family. Different, but maybe even better than her personal one. Had her district ever really let her down? Shamed her like her disparaging mother had? *Nee.* Much more so, she'd forsaken the community, treating individuals with envy, jealousy, ridicule and manipulation.

And when she'd been at her darkest, they'd shown up in droves. Lydia's heart swelled at the memory of the stream of buggies that had filled the hospital parking lot. Even Edna and Susie had hurried over when news of Caleb's fall had spread to their district.

Although her stomach was in knots as the service's last song wound to its protracted end, precipitating her impending confession, the fingers that stroked over Caleb's bare foot didn't tremble. She was looking at the upcoming event in a new light.

Confession in front of the church body, although anxiety inducing, was necessary. It showed the individual was subordinate to the group and it elevated *Gelassenheit.* Submission was a vital tenet of their faith. Submission to *Gott* and to the church. She had broken vows she'd made to both. Confession and repentance was the way toward redemption and reconnection.

The ministers would be seeking a response to a specific situation, but as Lydia looked around at the faces, there were oh, so many wrongs to make right and things she needed to confess. Her gaze landed on Jonah and quickly skipped away again. Particularly to one. To him, instead of confessing to an offense, of which there were many, she wanted to proclaim her love. If only doing so wouldn't hurt him in the long run even more than her lies.

He looked drawn. Had he slept as little as she had? Surely he'd heard about yesterday. Though he hadn't been there. Lydia sighed. She'd missed him. Throughout the ordeal, she'd longed to be held by him, supported by him. An incongruous desire, as she'd been the one to push him away.

The song's final unaccompanied notes faded away. Lydia's shoulders rose and fell on another deep breath. She could do this. She was ready to do this. She *needed* to do this. She would confess all. Her pulse reverberated in her ears. All but the thing closest to her heart.

While Malinda followed others her age out of the room when nonmembers were excused at the end of the service, Fannie refused to be lured from her seat beside Lydia. Called to come forward, Lydia gently scooted the little girl off her skirt so she could stand. Caleb clung so tightly to her—as he had since yesterday—Lydia was afraid she'd have to take him up front with her. As she made her way along the bench lined with solid-colored skirts under aprons, Rachel was able to coax the boy into her arms. On trembling legs, Lydia proceeded down the aisle.

Jonah's mouth was dry as he watched Lydia approach where the ministers were gathered in the center of the congregation. When she dropped to her knees, his stomach dropped in unison.

He'd been out of the district yesterday, helping a fellow young carpenter with a two-man job. Still licking his wounds from Lydia's rejection, he'd been glad of the excuse at the time. But as soon as he'd heard of Caleb's fall, he'd raced to the hospital, arriving to a parking lot empty of buggies. He'd rushed inside to the desk to inquire, only to be told they couldn't give him any information as he wasn't a listed family member. The reminder twisted in his gut like a continually turning knife.

Though he'd longed to rush over and ensure for himself that his son was all right, Jonah figured he wouldn't receive any better reception at Lydia's place. He'd had to satisfy himself with what Hannah and Gail had assured him regarding the boy, unaware they were speaking of their own nephew.

This morning, he'd scanned the women's benches as he'd entered church with the other single men, inhaling sharply enough at the sight of Lydia's pale face and the white tape on Caleb's head, that he'd drawn his companions' attention. Jonah ached to step over the benches, to gather both into his arms.

But Lydia would leave if he did.

Maybe he would be better off without her. Look at Peter, as she'd mentioned. Jonah's gaze found the man's grim profile as Peter sat ahead of him with the married men. Lydia's wedded sister had run off with another man. Would that be Lydia's future as well? Maybe finding another woman to share his life with, one without that family history, would be better. Jonah returned his attention to his son, who'd been curled into his mother's shoulder. The thought of a life with anyone else flew out of his mind as quickly as it'd flitted in. He'd seen something in Lydia. Something he'd fallen in love with before. And he'd fallen again, his love even strengthening upon her return.

Clenching his fists, Jonah fixed his gaze on Lydia's strained profile, on her quavering answers to the bishop's questions. He recalled when she'd made a confession to him, a painful one of how she'd felt responsible for her cousin's death. He remembered her lament that she damaged anything that was good. That was far from the truth. Look at his son. Healthy and content, the boy was wonderful, as he had a wonderful mother. Look how she'd willingly taken in her nieces, who were already blossoming in her care.

A buzz rippled through the attendance as two-year-old Fannie scrambled off the bench seat and ran up the aisle to kneel beside Lydia. Bishop Weaver frowned. Standing there in his role as minister, Lydia's father rubbed a hand over his mouth. Lydia's pale face twitched in a small smile, before she laid a hand on the girl's back. The little one nestled closer.

Nee. Lydia was not like her sister.

Was her fear that she was, the reason she wouldn't marry him? Jonah furrowed his brow.

What had she actually said? It wasn't that she *didn't* love him, but that she didn't *want* to.

Jonah's heart was hammering. *Ja*, she'd made mistakes, but she wasn't alone in making the one she was answering for now. She wouldn't be up there if it wasn't for him.

His throat tightened as she made tearful confessions and lowered her head. She shouldn't be up there alone. He curled his fingers around the edge of the bench on which he sat. If he stood, Lydia would leave with his son and he might not ever see either of them again. His knee started bouncing. If he stood, those in the district would know he'd broken his vows as well. His folks, his siblings, his church family, all would know he didn't deserve the good standing in which they held him.

Still, everything he wanted was there at the rail. But to commit to being with her and Caleb, he had to be willing to leave all else he held dear and start anew. He didn't want to leave his home. His jaw flexed. But where was his home? Was it here? Or with her? Jonah waited for the bricks to fall. For responsibilities and the desire to be irreproachable to anchor him here. For all that was known and safe and expected to outweigh the admittance of his failure and the uncertainty of an uncharted path.

Instead, a lightness like he'd never experienced swept through him. Let her take his son and go back East. He'd go with them.

Jonah jolted to his feet, startling seatmates on either side of him. Murmurs erupted as dark-clad knees of the occupants who shared his bench abruptly swept aside as Jonah made his way to the aisle. Murmurs that died down as congregation members straightened on their backless seats as he moved past the rows to join Lydia up front with the ministers and bishop. There was utter silence as he dropped to his knees beside her.

Lydia gaped at him, her eyes wide. Reaching out, Jonah covered her hand, where it was clenched in her lap.

Though his chest was tight, his voice was strong. "I want to confess I've failed. I want to make peace." He cleared his throat. "This woman bore my son, whom I am belatedly, but gladly claiming." There was a swell of whispers at his words before it was quickly hushed. Jonah drew in a deep breath, feeling tension, instead of increasing, seep out at his confession. "May God and the church have patience with me. I will strive to take better care in the future."

Her hand was still tensely fisted under his. Jonah's voice projected throughout the large room. Perhaps even those who were waiting outside could hear him. He didn't care. "And regarding the future, if she will have me, I will marry her. My son has a *wunderbar* mother and I know she will make me a *wunderbar* wife as well."

Lydia tried to slip her hand from beneath his. "The women in my family…" she whispered. "We're not capable of a happy union. You deserve one."

Jonah kept her hand captured, not by force, but by love. "I'm happy when I'm with you," he whispered back.

"You might not've known what my mother was like in private, but you saw what my sister was. That's what I'll be. That's who I am. I won't trap you in that kind of marriage." Her slender throat bobbed in a swallow. Her eyes, bruised from lack of sleep and shimmering with tears, held his. Jonah lightly stroked his thumb over her slender fingers. She reminded him of a fragile flower, trampled under circumstances, but still striving to bloom.

"You are not your sister. Nor your mother. You asked me once if I thought people could change. I loved you before. But that love is a faint shadow of the love and respect I have for the woman you have become."

Beneath his palm, her hand twitched.

Slowly, hesitantly, it turned upward to clasp his. Tightly.

Breath shuddered from her. "I'm afraid."

Jonah squeezed her hand. "Trust me. Trust us. Trust *Gott*."

"I'll probably be shunned."

"I guess we both will be then. Just think, we can sit at the same table. I'm not trapped. I'm where I want to be. Together with you." Glancing up, Jonah noted all the engrossed—and amused—faces.

He ducked his head again toward Lydia. "So I've told, which you warned me against. I guess I better pack up my tools. My place is with you and my son, wherever you are." He grinned. "I'm figuring they wouldn't mind an extra carpenter in Pennsylvania."

The tears that had been shimmering in her eyes began to trickle down her cheek. "What did I ever do to deserve you?"

"I don't know. You must've done something wrong. Or I did something right." Raising their entwined hands to his lips, he gently kissed the back of hers.

Rebecca's droll voice easily carried throughout the cavernous room. "For sure and certain, if we were expecting a confession today, we certainly got it."

Epilogue

After a final check of the items in the back of the hired van, Jonah gave a nod to the driver and shut the door with a solid *thunk*. He turned to the gathering who'd come to say farewell. With a smile on his face, he shook his head and strode the few steps necessary to loop an arm over his wife's shoulders. The joy at being able to do so would never recede.

"I thought we're only going to be gone for two weeks? You've packed for—and the goodbyes appear—like we're crossing the ocean and it'll be months, if not years, before we return."

"There are gifts for Mary, from us and others, in there. And some things to keep the children entertained during the journey and once we're in Pennsylvania. I'm so glad we're going to see her. I'm so glad she encouraged me to come back and make peace with my past." Lydia's eyes were shining as she eased Caleb, wide-eyed at all the activity, down to stand at her feet, supported by a fistful of her skirt.

"That makes two of us. I look forward to meeting her. I owe her a lot."

They watched Malinda and Fannie give their father another hug. Although time would tell if the disrupted family ever fully recovered, all three seemed much improved from Lucetta's departure six weeks ago. Peter was striving to reach a balance between fatherhood and work to support his family. Grateful for the adventure for the girls as he sorted things out, he'd happily agreed to the trip.

Neither Lydia, nor Jonah, had been banned. The church members—too diverted by the two-for-one confession and joking that Amish always enjoyed a bargain—had voted not to shun them. It was understandable. The couple had earnestly confessed and repented. They had been forgiven. And, as the deacon had stated that Jonah's announcement might as well serve as publishing their betrothal, they'd been married two weeks later in a subdued event.

Their ceremony had only preceded Henry and Edna's nuptials by a few weeks. That'd been part of the reason for the timing of this trip. To give the new arrivals a chance to get settled in their new home, with Henry and Edna in the *daadi haus*, which Jonah had finished in a flurry with the help of Josiah, and Susie in the main one.

When Jonah returned, he'd be leaving the dairy behind to plunge into his carpentry business in earnest. He might even hire Josiah or one of his other brothers part-time. Not because he enjoyed their company, but to keep them out of trouble, of course.

"What are we going to do when Jacob and his girl get married shortly after we get back? It's going to be a full house."

He smiled into Lydia's upturned face. "Someday I'll build us one of our own. In the meantime…" Eyeing the structure, Jonah rubbed his chin where a beard, marking him as a married man, was just beginning to grow in. "I guess I can add on in the other direction."

Lydia leaned her head on his shoulder. "Are you sorry you've taken on me and my family?"

Grinning at the tug on his trousers as Caleb transferred his grasp from his mother's skirt to cling to his father's pants, Jonah knelt to lift his son into his arms. Cradling the boy against one shoulder, Jonah pulled Lydia around to face him with the other and gently kissed her. He figured he was safe doing so publicly. Everyone else was still busy chatting.

"*Nee.* I think your family is just right. And as long as I have you both, everything else is as well."

* * * * *

Dear Reader,

One character I never expected to see again was Lydia Troyer. When she'd popped up in my earlier books, she'd been unpleasant to say the least, until after being particularly rude to one heroine, I'd sent her out of the area, figuring she would never return.

I had trouble warming up to her as a heroine at first, having previously made her quite disagreeable. But as I got to know her, and understand her, I discovered the person I'd thought I'd known wasn't who she was now. I am so glad that God, and others, give me grace when my actions might be those of a character that I'm tempted to write out of a story. And hopefully, I'm a grace giver to others. Maybe it is a good thing that Lydia returned to Miller's Creek, as I've learned so much from her journey.

To keep posted on where my journey is going or what might be happening next at Miller's Creek, you can follow me on Facebook at Author Jocelyn McClay or stop by my website at jocelynmcclay.com. Thanks so much for reading Jonah and Lydia's story!

May God Bless You,
Jocelyn